Christmas
H⒤MESTEAD

**Based on the Hallmark Channel Original Movie
Written By Rick Garman**

Kara Tate

ISBN: 978-1-947892-11-8

www.hallmarkpublishing.com
For more about the movie visit:
www.hallmarkchannel.com/christmas-in-homestead

TABLE OF CONTENTS

CHAPTER ONE

As Jessica McEllis rode in the back of her custom, tinted-window town car to her home in a chic, gated community of Los Angeles, she rested easy in knowing exactly how blessed she was to have the life she did.

It was what she'd been working toward for years, and now all her dreams were coming true. She was at the top of her game as an actress and about to start her new adventure and climb the next rung on her career ladder: Producer.

She'd strived to get here and, well, so what if she'd given up certain things to achieve her dreams? No one got everything they wanted.

But, a little privacy would be nice occasionally. Sometimes she felt... tired.

Like right now as she returned from a meeting with her agent.

As her driver-slash-bodyguard-slash-superhero, Gavin, pulled up to the gate of her posh home, he had to slow down to avoid hitting the gaggle of paparazzi hoping to catch a good shot of her and maybe even a word or two.

Sure, sometimes the fame could take a toll in a way Jessica had never expected. But it was that same fame and success that enabled her to pick and choose which stories she wanted to tell. And this new movie was her most exciting venture yet.

The car rolled to a stop to let the gate slip open.

"Jessica! Jessica!" The photo-shooting life-chasers were respectful enough to not get aggressive and pound on the car.

They'd always treated her well—or as well as you could treat someone whose life you used to get paid. She tried to remember they were just doing their job and to handle them fairly in return. Hollywood was a tough world. She got it. She didn't have to like it, but she got it.

After all, not many people had the opportunities and lifestyle these compromises afforded her. She traveled the world, met interesting people, and posed for some of the top photographers. Dealing with paparazzi was just the other part of the job description.

Focusing on the good in her life helped her smile through the invasion of her privacy. It was what she did. Every day. Jess placed the camera-ready, friendly grin on her face as she lowered the window.

"Hi, guys. Good to see you, as always." She did a quick scan of the group, filled with the usual suspects and a few more hoping to grab a great shot of her before the new movie.

"Jessica!" Ian Carter, who had always been ambitious but kind, shouted, waving his free hand to get her attention. "We saw Vince Hawkins arrive. What's it like doing another film with your ex-boyfriend?"

She'd known that would be a popular question when she'd cast her ex in the role of the innkeeper to her movie star. Star-crossed lovers of the modern type. She just hadn't thought she'd hear the same question quite this often.

She was also for world peace, against global warming, and pro-classic pencil skirts, but no one ever asked her about those.

"*Ex*-boyfriend, guys. Keyword here is *ex*." She gave them her best sassy grin to let them know it was all in fun—no hard feelings—then sent the focus back to where she wanted it: the movie. "It's going to be a great film."

And that was all that mattered. She'd agreed to bring Vince on because they worked well together and had amazing on-screen chemistry. She needed the best chance at success she could get with her first film as a producer and was willing to take whatever measures she had to. Even if that meant dealing with the celebrity gossip hounds creating un-stories about her and her co-star.

She flashed the photographers another warm smile and started to roll up her window before giving them all a little wave. The continued shouts of her name echoed in the car as she collapsed back against the rich leather seats. It was time to put her producer hat on now that she'd gotten her actress duties out of the way.

"Gavin." She leaned forward to talk to her bodyguard as he pulled up to her front door. "We're definitely heading into new territory with this one."

He flashed her a wide smile in the rearview mirror and nodded his agreement.

Oh, Gavin. You chatty fellow, you.

Before getting out of the car, she straightened her skirt and pulled it as low as she could. She had no interest in being the next accidental flasher and going viral with her panties showing. Those super-powered lenses meant always being hyper-cognizant. That awareness had become second nature. One slip-up early in her career, when she'd accidentally tucked her skirt into her panties and had ended up on a celebrity gossip site, had trained her well.

Gavin came around and opened the door, doing his best to screen her from view as she slid out. As shields went, Gavin was more like a wall, actually. Standing over six feet two inches, his bulk was intimidating enough. But his drown-in-them dark brown eyes and gorgeous smile made him look like the action star version of a bodyguard as much as the real deal.

All this had made him the obvious choice to play her bodyguard in the new movie.

The look Gavin had given her had said it all. His gift with looks was particularly helpful since Gavin was a man of few words. Actually, most of the time, he was a man of *no* words.

Jessica gave another wave down the drive and headed toward the house, pulling off her hat as she went. It was good to be home. Her house was a sanctuary. The true center of her world away from prying eyes and being Public Jessica. Everything how she liked it, clean lines, organized. A place where she had complete control.

A place where there was suddenly a huge, beautifully decorated Christmas tree.

Behind her, Gavin stopped, obviously taking in the new addition as well. At least, she'd like to think he was wondering what in the world it was doing in her living room, since that was exactly what she was thinking.

"Jess!" Rosalie, her publicist, stood, Christmas ball in hand, in front of the room's new addition. "What do you think?"

"Rosalie, what is that?" Jessica motioned to the tree, even though she was pretty sure Rosalie must know the huge pine-scented thing in her living room was the obvious issue.

"It's a Christmas tree." Rosalie flashed her a stunning smile and waved the ornament in her hand a bit before finding a home for it on the tree.

"Yes." Well, ask a silly question... "It's beautiful. Why is it in my house?"

Rosalie set the next decoration down and turned to Jessica. She continued to smile, but it looked a bit forced. "Because it's almost Christmas." She waved a hand toward the tree, beautiful and perfect, just like all of Rosalie's handiwork. "Everyone needs a tree."

Jessica glanced around and couldn't help feeling like she was killing the joy as she wondered why in the world she needed a tree. In *her* house. Rosalie had obviously taken great care with it, creating a masterpiece any celebrity magazine would be more than thrilled to add to their holiday spreads.

But still.

Jess stepped into the room, joining Rosalie, and placed a hand on her shoulder, trying to lessen the sting of her response.

"We're spending the next ten days in Iowa shooting a Christmas movie. I'll see plenty of trees there."

"Yeah, but..." Rosalie glanced over her shoulder and lowered her voice. "You're producing and starring in the movie. How much tree-enjoyment, holiday-spirit time will you get?"

"Probably a lot, since it's a Christmas movie." And again, Iowa. Lots of trees.

"Okay." Rosalie shook her head, obviously not letting go of her hope of a Holiday Spirit taking over the event. "Your co-star awaits you for the meeting. Barbara just texted. She's two minutes away."

Not exactly what Jessica wanted to hear. Things went smoothly when people were on time. Plans mattered. Plans got things done, and being a strong planner had gotten her this far—producing at thirty wasn't something to sneeze at.

"Thanks. But a director who runs late…" She shook it off. No reason to get off on the wrong foot. Barbara was a pro, and she'd make it work. "Okay, let's do this so I can pack and get on the road."

Rosalie gave a little shake of her head, probably laughing at Jessica's need for order. "I'll wait for Barbara."

Which was exactly what Jessica needed. She had other issues to deal with, and it was probably best to handle them without an audience—especially an audience completely made up of the movie's future director.

She took a deep breath and went to handle Vince Hawkins, Mr. Hollywood's Most Eligible Bachelor—at least, he was since their breakup. Hopefully, they'd work together with the same magic they'd had before.

And if not, she'd figure that out, too.

In the game room at the back of the house, she found him playing billiards by himself—and, of course, dressed like a *GQ* fashion shoot was happening around him.

He glanced up, giving her a once-over.

"That's a nice tree upstairs." He flashed her his signature smile. "Whose is it?"

"What do you mean, whose is it?" She tried not to get defensive, but leave it to Vince to rock the boat as soon as she walked in the room. "It's mine."

"Yeah, right." Vince gave her a look that clearly stated he didn't even believe her a little bit before sending yet another one of his grins her way. "Since when do you get a tree?"

The need to justify her unwanted tree had her digging in her heels. It was in her house, it was Christmas, and she was not going to let Vince come in here and make her feel defensive.

"Since— Well, I felt like it."

"Ah." Vince leaned against the billiards table, going into full flirt mode. "But who needs a tree when they'll be in Fiji again for Christmas with...?"

He drew the word out, and Jessica knew exactly what he was getting at. Vince seemed to be having a rough time letting go of this dating relationship. He was treating the pre-production meetings like business as usual for them.

But it wasn't. Not even a little. They were friends now—*just* friends—and she needed him to get that. She had wanted more than what their relationship had offered. They both deserved more, even as she still valued the friendship they'd developed before they'd changed it to a romantic one.

"Her best girlfriend?" Jessica tried not to roll her eyes and placed a hand on Vince's arm. "Vince, you and I broke up. Jill is going to Fiji in your place this year."

She kept having to have these conversations with him.

He'd even told one media outlet two months ago they were just on a break.

"Ouch." He winced. "Good for Jill, though."

He took a step closer, forcing Jess to stand her ground as he shifted right back into handsome-leading-man persona.

Before she could swing them into work mode, he went on. "So, does that mean we should keep things strictly professional on location?"

That was a bud to nip immediately, and not just because of the no-longer-dating part of the conversation.

"This is my first time producing a movie." She tried to keep the nerves out of her voice. Vince would do an amazing job and have her back, but she wanted to be confident, professional—and taken seriously. "My first big thing after the *Asterlight* series, and I can't let anything mess that up."

"Classic Jessica." Vince added a smirk to his nod.

"What does that mean?" Coming from Vince, that definitely didn't sound like a compliment.

"You always have a detailed plan for everything."

Again, not a compliment.

"No, I don't." Okay, maybe she did. But that wasn't a bad thing.

Vince had accused her more than once of being a control freak who made him live by her detailed plans.

"Do so!"

She took a step back. Five-year-olds had more mature arguments than this.

"Well, excuse me, Mr. Play-everything-by-ear." She squared her shoulders, trying to make herself bigger to match his size and ability to loom over her. Not that he'd ever use that advantage on her. Vince was secretly a teddy bear.

They'd always bickered. It was often how they communicated. But, while Cary Grant and Katharine Hepburn were adorable when they did it on-screen, it wasn't always as much fun off-screen.

He paused, leaning into her space.

"You know,"—Vince grinned, waggling his eyebrows a bit—"if this were a movie, this would be the part where we kiss."

"Do you see a camera?" She was *so* done with this conversation.

He flipped his phone out of his pocket with a not-so-subtle, "Bam!" and another waggle of the brows. Jessica shook her head, smiling. Vince wasn't just a charmer, he was truly charming. He'd always known how to lighten her moods. It was one of the balances that made them a good team.

"Come on. Truce?" He tapped a finger on his cheek. "It will be good PR for the movie."

Jess rolled her eyes. There he went pushing exactly the right buttons again to get her to do what he wanted. The movie's success was vital to her. She loved the story and was proud to make this her first producer gig.

"Fine." She leaned into to kiss his cheek, surprised—and yet on some level, not—when he turned his head at the last second and snapped the pic. "Vince!"

Vince flashed her a grin, that smile that let him get

away with too much for too long from way too many people. "This will look great on Instagram."

"That is not funny." This was the last thing she needed while trying to juggle all the other pre-production tasks and meetings. A personal PR nightmare. "I'm not kidding. Delete that."

"Oh, come on."

"No." Jess knew when to put her foot down. With Vince, that was pretty much always.

He gave her a long look then shook his head as if he were thinking about it before flashing that get-away-with-anything grin again.

"Fine." Vince flipped to the pic, holding it up for her to see with his other hand.

She should have known better than to just walk away.

Chapter Two

Matt Larson didn't need the Homestead Holiday Celebration Christmas Countdown banner in the town square to tell him there were twelve days to go.

He loved Christmas. He loved the traditions, the family gatherings, and the town coming together even more than they did the rest of the year. He even almost loved the town squabbles.

Okay. Maybe not those.

What he was *not* loving was this phone call with his father.

"You and Mom are going where?" Matt knew he couldn't have heard his dad correctly. It was Christmas. Christmas might as well be taglined: Time for Family.

"Europe. Your mother has always wanted to go, but running the inn meant no long trips." His dad's smile all but came through the phone. "But now that you and Zoe are in charge, we're free to take this opportunity to see more of the world."

"But a river cruise in Europe?" Matt was trying to keep his cool, but how could his father not see what he was doing here? "What about Christmas? What am I going to tell Zoe and Sophie?"

His sister, Zoe, slipped into the lobby at the sound of her name. "Tell me and Sophie what?"

He sucked in a breath, not excited to be the bearer of bad news. "Mom and Dad won a raffle. They're skipping Christmas to do a cruise." Matt tried not to sound too annoyed since his dad could still hear him, but his success level was low at best.

"Cool! Give it to me." Zoe snatched the phone from Matt before he could step away, her excitement clear in her tone. "Dad? We're very happy. Yes, even Matt is happy. Aren't you, big brother?" Zoe turned toward him, giving him a look only a sister could get away with.

As opposites went, he and his free-spirited sister were as far apart as you could get.

He tried to stay out of it, to not be upset. But he still couldn't help how he felt as he muttered, "I'm not. I'm really not."

Zoe shook her head at him as if he were going to be happy for them just because she said to.

"Ow." When Zoe pinched him, he knew he'd have to cave. Change wasn't his favorite thing, but arguing with his dad ranked even lower. He leaned toward the phone and raised his voice. "Yes. We're very happy."

"See? No." Zoe shook her head. "Don't worry

about the lodge. That's why you left the business to us—so you can go gallivanting around the globe."

Matt wasn't so sure anyone should be gallivanting anywhere, especially during the holidays, but he was obviously outvoted. He watched Zoe wander off, phone at her ear, babbling about the lodge and the potential fun his parents would have in Europe.

She was, in so many ways, his opposite—easy-going, light-hearted, and always ready to roll with whatever life sent her. They got along well, but that didn't mean they always agreed. Actually, it meant they seldom agreed on anything, except the important stuff, like family. And Christmas.

Which was why he was so confused about how well she was handling their parents being away.

He stood, thinking about how to make Christmas special with some of his loved ones on the other side of the ocean. This wasn't the first time he'd had to adjust to loss at the holidays—it was just the first time he'd lost to a raffle prize.

From the main room, a loud roar and music better suited to an epic saga than a country inn flowed. But when the ring of metal on metal sounded, he headed in that direction—pronto.

The parlor was his favorite room on the guest side. Right now, not only the parlor, but the entire lodge was decorated with homey furnishings, a fireplace with stockings, a Christmas tree... and his ten-year-old daughter who sat rapt on the couch, her light brown braids partially obscuring her face, watching a movie on her iPad.

"Hey, Sophie." Matt dropped down next her, remembering again how blessed he was. "What are you watching?"

"*The Asterlight Chronicles Part Three: The Fires of Smeed!* " Sophie gave him just a little look, barely glancing away from the screen in her hand.

Ah, the father-daughter bonding Matt was always so proud of. He and Sophie were as close as two peas in a pod—if there wasn't an iPad movie playing within reaching distance.

"That's the movie about the dragons?" *Please let it be the dragons.*

Matt realized immediately he'd guessed wrong. Sophie rolling her eyes almost all the way back in her head was his first clue.

"*Dad.* It's not really dragons." She offered him a look of disdain as only a young girl truly can and readied herself to explain the importance of *Asterlight.* "It's about this girl, Helena Asterlight, who saves the world."

Well, that was something. A good message. He was happy she was watching stuff about girl power if she was going to glue herself to a screen. He'd seen the reports about girls and media, so that was one concern he could set aside for today.

Matt glanced down at his daughter, his heart rushing to his throat. He was doing the best he could without his wife, Melanie. Since they'd lost her, he'd been blessed to have Zoe step in and help on the girl stuff and general aunt love. His own little family. One day, Zoe, with her over-sized aspirations and desires, might head out on her own adventures, but for now, the three of them made a darn good team.

He really didn't think he could take any more change right now anyway. So Zoe was staying put, even if he had to tie her to something unmovable.

Glancing back down at the iPad in Sophie's hands, he watched a woman stride to the front of the screen while drawing a sword.

"Who's that?" The woman stood in the middle of the shot, backlit by a light so bright she was almost haloed, her weapon pointing forward.

He apparently finally had Sophie's attention with that one question.

"That's Jessica McEllis! She's like the most famous, prettiest actress in the world." Sophie paused the movie, sucking in another big breath before continuing. "And she's gonna be staying here, in our lodge! Isn't that cool?"

Hollywood wasn't even here yet and they were already invading.

"Yeah. Cool." Matt was not impressed with the actress who would be taking over his town during the most important week of the year. But that wasn't even his biggest concern right now. Breaking it to Sophie that her Nana and Papa weren't coming home for Christmas was. "Can you shut that off? I need to talk to you."

"Dad!"

"Daughter!" He tried rolling his eyes at her, but apparently, that only worked on older generations. She reluctantly set aside her iPad, and he decided to break it to her quickly.

"Thank you." He took a deep breath. This wasn't news he was excited about sharing. If he was struggling with his parents not coming home, he couldn't imagine how his daughter would feel. "Okay. So. Your grandma and grandpa aren't coming home for Christmas."

Sophie's eyes grew big, rounding out as she finally gave him her full attention. He wasn't sure how he was going to make this up to her. It was going to be okay. He'd *make* it okay. Matt's mind was already racing with ways to create an even more special Christmas season than usual.

Hopefully, ways that did not involve more staring at a screen.

Sophie sucked in a distraught breath. "But they're going to miss—"

"Christmas morning, opening the presents in our pajamas..." He leaned back, settling in next to her, then wrapping an arm around her. "I know."

"No!" Sophie leaned back, the upset on her face obvious. She was taking this worse than he had expected. "They're going to miss meeting Jessica!"

Matt froze, unsure how to manage that. The upside was she was going to handle absentee grandparents for the first time over the holidays okay.

But... was he the only person who cared about Christmas and family time anymore?

Apparently, because Sophie picked her iPad up again to drown her sorrow in the dragon movie that wasn't about dragons.

He gave Sophie a kiss on the head and made his exit before he found himself trying to explain life and the holidays to his ten-year-old.

He was going to embrace the Christmas spirit even if it killed him.

Matt wandered to the far side of the front room, glancing out at the town as it was starting to pull together the holiday decorations.

Behind him, he could still hear the sound of *Asterlight* and Zoe's conversation with their dad. Neither of those were things he wanted to listen to.

Tuning everything out, he studied the lodge's decorations, making sure everything was just as it should be before the next group of guests arrived. He may not want the movie coming to town, but that didn't mean that Homestead Lodge wouldn't always offer every guest their very best.

Matt stepped back from the Christmas tree perfectly decorated with handmade ornaments, enjoying having everything in the absolute right place. It wasn't just for himself he liked these special touches—although, the holidays were always important. And not just because of the family time and love of the holiday, either, but because Melanie had loved it.

Keeping that love alive in his house was too important to slack on. For himself. For Sophie.

And, as an innkeeper, he had a great excuse, because it was important for his guests, too.

He let his eyes drop shut as he listened to the battle sounds coming out of Sophie's iPad. He really needed to do something about that thing.

"Okay. I will." Zoe wandered into the living room, cell phone still at her ear. "Love you. Bye."

He tried not to let his gut shift as she hung up with their parents. He was an adult, for goodness' sake. He didn't need his mom and dad coming to hold his hand at Christmas.

He just wanted them to be there. Because… family.

"Soph, we have to go to the town meeting before the tree lighting ceremony." Zoe stuck the phone in her pocket, as much focused on him as his daughter. "Go get your coat, 'kay?"

Sophie tucked her tablet under her arm and headed out to grab her stuff. Matt knew what was coming, even as he stood by the tree pretending it wasn't.

"Be happy for Mom and Dad."

"I am." He should definitely work on his enthusiasm. Instead, he jumped back, avoiding yet another one of Zoe's killer pinches. Brother abuse should be reportable. "I am! I just…"

"You aren't good with change," she finished for him.

"That's not true." His family—heck, the whole

town—knew he'd adjusted, adapted, and dealt with more change than a man his age should have to.

"Is this about the movie?" Zoe leaned over and bumped his shoulder. "Or Melanie?"

Matt took a deep breath, sucking it in and tasting all the goodness squeezed into their little lodge—the fresh smell of pine, the cookies baking in the kitchen, whatever quirky scent Zoe was wearing today. All of it was centering. Real.

But Zoe kept going. "Christmas was always her favorite time of the year."

He stepped away. It was not a conversation he needed today. He'd already had enough smile-and-nod conversations with the two ladies in his life for one afternoon.

"I'm fine with change when something needs changing." He glanced down at his watch, thankful for a valid conversation-ender. "We'd better go. The mayor shouldn't be late for his own town meeting."

He wrapped his arm around his sister, pulling her into a side hug as he walked her to the door.

He was a lucky man—even when he wasn't. This was the time of year to count his blessings.

Blessing number one: his annoying, nosy sister with a heart of gold.

CHAPTER THREE

People who knew Jessica well might assume that she'd be feeling a little impatient about her director being on the phone instead of doing director-y stuff.

She was trying desperately to prove those people wrong.

Even if they never knew it.

Twenty minutes later, Jessica was ready to get things started. They were two days away from starting to shoot scenes in Homestead, and making sure all her ducks were in a row was at the top of her list.

What Vince had said about her needing to have everything in its box had hit a nerve. Not that there was anything wrong with things being in their right boxes. But if she was the boss, she didn't want to be That Boss.

Instead, she took the free moments to walk Vince through the settings that were already going to be in place because of shooting on location.

"That's the inn and that's the town square." She pointed to each of the location shots spread out on the table, her excitement ramping back up after seeing what the town did before the crew even brought in the set dressings.

"And that's a candy cane and that's a nutcracker," Vince added, pointing to the oversized yard decorations.

She typically loved when Vince broke the tension on set with his humor, but now she was feeling bad for every producer and director who had ever worked with them as a team.

He went to point out a snowman, and she slapped his hand away, trying to figure out how to keep him on task.

Maybe she should promise him cookies like her parents did when—*if*—she behaved.

Just as she was about to lose her patience, she glanced up as Barbara McKeevers rushed in, trying valiantly to get off the phone.

"Trevor, I don't care if she made fun of your turtle, and the turtle doesn't care, either. Now, be good. Love you. Bye." She huffed a breath into the phone as she pulled it away from her ear and hit *end*.

Glancing at Jessica, Barbara gave her a look she couldn't quite read. It wasn't apologetic, but she followed it up with a "Sorry."

"It's okay." Kids. That wasn't something she was used to dealing with. She loved kids, but most of the casts she'd typically been part of were women in their twenties—sneaking into their thirties. And Hollywood, no matter what their Instagrams tried to tell you, still had men catering to their fans with pictures of kids but very little in terms of responsibilities.

She glanced toward Barbara, realizing that this movie was different. Now, sitting in the driver's seat, Jess was second-guessing and wondering about things that wouldn't have even registered on her radar before.

"So." Jessica tried to keep the conversation light but couldn't help worrying about her director's family arrangements. "How are the kids going to handle you going on location?"

"Oh, it'll be *Lord of the Flies*, but that's my husband's problem." Barbara paused and glanced around the room as if weighing her options and not really sure she was coming up the winner. "My problem will be ten days of outdoor shoots in December in Iowa."

"No kidding."

Jessica was afraid to admit that was exactly what she wanted to hear. The reassurance that Barbara was focused on the movie bolstered Jess that she was right when she'd insisted Barbara was the woman she wanted for this story.

The tale of a starlet who falls for—and has to leave—an innkeeper outside her Hollywood world was both beautiful and heartbreaking. Her instinct had told her that a woman would tell this particular story the best. And when she'd met Barbara, she'd known that woman was her.

Jess wrapped her in a quick hug and settled down at the table to run through the details of the coming week. The location photos were adorable. The town was even better than anything that she could have had created on a sound set.

She was a *Gilmore Girls* fan—because who wasn't?—and it was as if someone had thought to bring Stars Hollow to life then decorated for Christmas.

She'd have to remember to send a big thank you note to the location scouts. She couldn't wait to see it in person.

The script pages were going through a final, pre-location vetting, and the schedule looked solid. No surprises on the horizon. Just how she liked it.

"Wait, my itinerary says you're going up tomorrow?" Barbara seemed surprised but not concerned over her involvement.

Jessica jumped in, not wanting Barbara to think she was overstepping.

"My character grew up there." She glanced again at the detail sheet for her character, a famous actress who had returned home for the holidays. She was playing a prodigal and was thrilled with the idea. "I want to get a feel for the place."

And a little downtime before getting started. A few moments to settle in and be ready to go when everyone else got there wouldn't hurt, either.

"I don't need to get a feel for the place." Vince's confidence had always been attractive… until it wasn't. "I'm playing an innkeeper, so it's not rocket science. I know because I played a rocket scientist who saved the world."

He grinned at Jessica, and she didn't even bother to fight the look she gave him in return. She certainly still adored Vince… in a brother-who-must-be-humored-at-all-times type of way, but, really?

"Yes, Vince." Jessica patted him on the arm. "That's exactly the same."

Jess could at least thank him for the bonding moment with Barbara as both women shared a look over the rocket-scientist-turned-innkeeper logic.

Guys—they certainly had their own reality rules.

Barbara turned back to her very thick binder of logistics.

"We'll need to be done by the twenty-third." Barbara paged through the schedule one more time, making sure everything lined up exactly right. "My family will notice if I'm not there on Christmas Eve."

Jessica nodded, more to herself than Barbara. They were cutting it close, but this was how Hollywood worked. Everyone wanted perfection on the smallest budget possible. But filming in this location during the holidays was an advantage. She'd seen the photos from the previous years and couldn't help but feel the holiday spirit seeping through them.

On the other side of the table, Vince nodded along as Barbara ran him through some scene notes. Sometimes it was hard to tell he was a rock-hard professional. But under his charm and playfulness, she knew everything Barbara was saying was not only sinking in, but shifting his approach to the role.

As Jess watched, Rosalie leaned over her shoulder,

casually acting like she was looking on with what she was doing. Until Rosalie sprung her latest suggestion on her. "What about spending Christmas with your folks?"

Jessica should have seen it coming, but she'd hoped after the whole tree thing, Rosalie would be done with the holiday suggestions.

"I'm taking Jill to Fiji." Jess turned to the next schedule, double-checking the numbers. "She just broke up with her boyfriend."

"I'm just asking." Rosalie was never *just* asking. "I'm sure your folks would love to see you."

And apparently, guilt was her weapon of choice this time.

"I'd love to see them, too." A flash of homesickness she hadn't felt in years rushed through her. "But I bring too much drama with me. Plus, I already told them I can't come."

And the fact that they always seemed fine with her absence was something she left unspoken. Rosalie didn't need to know that her relationship with her parents had diminished the more popular she became. They not only weren't in love with her career of choice, but they downright hated the issues it brought along with it.

She couldn't really blame them. Hollywood was definitely its own world, but the disappointment of separating herself further from her family was the ultimate downside.

She glanced up, shifting back to work mode and dragging Rosalie along with her.

"We're good with the town?" As if they had a choice at this point. Homestead was the location no matter what since they were starting in two days—but she needed to know what they were walking into and how she could smooth the way if the location manager hadn't managed to already. "Someone said the mayor wasn't happy."

"They have these Christmas events, and he doesn't want us in the way." Rosalie smiled an apology, obviously not excited about being the messenger of bad news.

Before Jessica could follow up about the events and their schedule, Barbara shifted around to join them. "But that's why we want to film in this town."

She'd read all about Barbara's immersion tactics in the past and wasn't surprised that she wanted the flavor of their film already in place before they even started their own layering of the holiday look and feel.

"I'd think they'd be excited." Jess ran through every location shoot she'd ever done in her head. Had there been issues before and she just hadn't realized it? What did the producers do then? But why would people care? It seemed like such a win-win. "I mean, think of the publicity. Right?"

Everyone kind of shrugged it off. There was no making sense of non-movie people. Didn't they know publicity like that meant income for the shops and the town? Tourism would shoot up, as would the ability to raise their prices. It could turn a small town like Homestead into a destination spot if their movie went huge.

Jess started compiling a list of locations that had benefited from being story locations. Forks in Washington, Tombstone in Arizona... the list was wide and long.

She settled back to watch her team get to work. They were going to rock this, then the whole town would fall in love with them and the newfound popularity the shoot bought their corner of the world.

Matt patted his coat pocket where he had tucked the last meeting's notes and his agenda for this one. Of course, he had his notebook that Pete Steverson insisted stay at City Hall, but these were *his* notes— ideas, plans, questions that had come up.

And if ever he needed to come prepared with notes, it was this month.

He waited until Zoe and Soph joined him in the foyer to head outside.

"Ready?" He pulled the door shut behind them, posting their placard that read: *Welcome to Homestead Lodge. We'll be back at...*

He filled in 4 p.m., but then, after a knowing look from Zoe, changed the sign to read 5 p.m. instead. They headed down the front stairs, Sophie wrapping her mittened hand in his.

"It's freezing out here." Zoe was swathed in one of her cute jackets and matching gloves but probably still not layered enough. "When we franchise and start opening other lodges, the first one is going to be someplace warm."

Matt ignored everything about that statement, except that it was cold. He nodded at that because... true fact.

Sophie did not.

"We're opening another lodge?" she asked, probably running through every scenario she could come up with.

Matt gave Zoe a look over Sophie's head. That's all he needed was his daughter thinking they'd be moving at a moment's notice. "No. We're not."

"Yes, we are. Someday." Zoe shot him a smug glare that clearly said his vote was not going to matter. "I didn't get a degree in hotel management just so I could help run my parents' lodge forever."

Why couldn't everyone appreciate what they had? He glanced around again at the magically lit-up town square. They had so much here.

"So, Soph," Matt jumped back in, changing the subject because walking to a town meeting wasn't the place for this conversation. "Who else is in the movie?"

Sophie hopped from foot to foot, tugging on his hand. He'd obviously landed on the right topic.

"Vince Hawkins!" At her dad's blank look, Sophie let out a long-suffering sigh and went on to educate him. "The action star. Dad, you should know this."

He grinned at her, trying to remember being so young that the only important things in your life were if your best friend was free for a ballgame and your favorite action star.

"I don't have time for celebrity stuff." He side-hugged her to him as they dodged a light post wrapped up like a candy cane. "I'm busy raising a kid, running the lodge, and being mayor."

"They're staying at our lodge." Sophie let out an exasperated sigh to rival an eighty-year-old busybody aunt. "You should know everything about them."

"I don't know everything about any of our other guests." He refrained from pointing out the stalker-ness of her statement because she was ten. But still.

Sophie was having none of that. "Dad, if you embarrass me in front of the movie stars—"

"Don't worry, Sophie," Zoe jumped in. "I'll make sure he doesn't do anything dumb."

It was tough being the only man in the family, so Matt let that go, too.

But since his daughter was so interested in this actress and her movies, he should probably find out more about them. "Are there dragons in the movie they're doing here?"

"I just can't." Sophie shook head, obviously giving up on her father like only a teenager could. Thank goodness that phase was still a few years away.

Matt grinned to himself. She was adorable even at her feistiest. Just like her mom had been.

He listened to Zoe and Sophie chatter for the rest

of the walk, enjoying the way they fit together and their banter.

When they got to the Town Hall, the entire main room was packed. People were already milling around inside, drinking cider, and munching away on decorated Christmas cookies. There was an unanticipated buzz of excitement in the air.

Why hadn't he been able to get this many people to attend the meeting about changing the Thompson Street yield sign to a stop sign last year?

Matt kissed Sophie on the head before leaving her with Zoe and taking his place at the podium with the city council.

After an hour, even Matt was sick of the meeting, and he typically loved them. Pete Steverson, the lead councilman, stood at the podium, discussing the upcoming Hollywood invasion. Couldn't people see they weren't "Hollywood" here? Small towns were small for a reason.

When Pete stopped to take a breath and move on to the next movie-related item—how to harness the publicity—Matt couldn't take it anymore.

"We don't want the publicity," he interjected.

"Mr. Mayor—"

"Pete," Matt jumped in to have the same conversation they'd been having since he'd been elected, "you've known me since I was born. Call me Matt."

"Mr. Mayor," Pete went on as if he hadn't spoken, "this issue has already been decided by the town council."

Matt didn't care what had been decided. He cared about the town and what was best for it.

"But the tree lighting, the snowman building, the carriage rides..." Matt glanced around, imploring them with everything he had to hold tight to the things and events that made Homestead, Homestead. "These are our town's traditions. Isn't that what Christmas is all about? I mean, what's more important? A bunch of movie stars coming in and taking over the town... or our families?"

He looked out into the crowd, hoping they'd been won over by his reminders of all the joys they had at the holidays.

"I want the movie stars," Sophie spoke up at him from the front row.

A cheer went up behind her as everyone shouted their agreement, and Matt watched people who he had always believed shared his values decide to sell out Christmas for the sake of meeting some famous people. And, on top of that, they weren't even willing to say it. Apparently, it took his ten-year-old daughter to stand up to him publicly to get them what they wanted.

"Meeting adjourned." Pete's gavel came down, slamming onto the podium next to him before Matt could take up his protest again. "Let's go light the tree!"

Everyone who'd just voted to destroy Christmas leapt up and rushed toward one of the very traditions Matt was trying to protect. How could he keep Homestead safe once Hollywood arrived?

That evening, knowing the tree-lighting might be their last tradition free from the outside world, Matt took special interest in making the event perfect. He had to weave through the crowd to catch up with the traitors—his daughter and sister. They were already standing at the edge of the circle, listening to the town choir finish a lovely version of "Hark, the Herald Angels Sing." Not only did the singers sound perfect, they looked amazing, decked out in their period costumes and backlit by the white lights in the snow. Beside them, Pete seemed as happy as anyone to have the tradition safely following its typical path.

As the choir drew to a close, Matt made his way to the stairs of the bandstand to look out over the crowd that had come to enjoy hot chocolate, carols, and the yearly tree-lighting.

"Thank you, Homestead Choir. That was beautiful, as always." Matt gave a moment for everyone to cheer, stepping back from the mic for an instant to enjoy the overall holiday vibe and town love. "Okay, let's kick off the Homestead Holidays with the lighting of the tree! Doing the honors this year is none other than my daughter... Sophie Larson."

Sophie walked up to the front of the group and joined him on the stairs, waving to the crowd as if it were her due.

"You ready?"

"I'm ready." She leaned against him, giving him a

moment for just the two of them. "Merry Christmas, Dad."

"Merry Christmas, Sophie."

Then, using a dramatic sweep of her hand, she pushed the button and the tree lit up, dazzling the crowd with its flickering lights. Pete waved everyone down to a hush and began making announcements about the various events to come.

With everything in order again, Matt put all worries of the Hollywood invasion behind him. At least for tonight.

CHAPTER FOUR

J essica ran through a list of everything she'd want to take with her to Homestead. She couldn't afford to forget anything. Did they even have major department stores up there? It looked fairly isolated on the map.

And what if she forgot something like her script notes? She wasn't just acting on this one. She needed to nail it. She double-checked that she had her notes, her script, her schedule, her production contact list.

Of course, Rosalie probably had all of that, too, but better safe than sorry.

Rosalie came up beside her with one more suitcase. Okay, maybe she hadn't forgotten anything since it looked like she was bringing everything. Gavin was definitely getting a workout loading the trunk.

He grabbed the last one and took it out while Rosalie ran through her typical departure checklist.

"Are you almost good to go?" Rosalie slung her

carry-on bag over her shoulder and tucked both her phones into her purse.

Jessica glanced around, about to leave the safety of her house for a challenge she could only pray she was up for.

"What if I mess it up?" Could anything be worse? She'd fought the cliché of being the more-looks-than-talent starlet face for years. "What if I'm always just the pretty girl who did the *Asterlight* movies?"

Maybe that.

"Hey, you're more than just the pretty girl." Rosalie ran a hand down her arm, giving it a quick, encouraging squeeze. "You're Jessica McEllis, slayer of dragons. Slay this one."

She watched Rosalie head out to the car, obviously feeling surer about the success of this Christmas story than Jessica did.

But it was time to head out there and make things happen. Turning off the lights, she couldn't help but notice as the little white bulbs on the tree flickered out.

They rode to the airport, going over last-minute items again to make sure everyone was comfortable with the plan. Typically, Jessica flew first class. But because of the multiple connecting flights and odd hours to get to Homestead, she'd hired a small private jet for her and her team.

It felt frivolous—but necessary.

As Gavin directed the luggage and ensured everything was on schedule and paparazzi free, Jessica texted her friend Jill to solidify the Fiji trip.

"You know, I'm really looking forward to Fiji with Jill." She glanced over at Rosalie, wanting her to understand it was more than just a second-best plan. "I'm going to need the downtime and drama-free zone even more when this two-week shoot is over."

"It's probably for the best." Rosalie gave her a smile before easing out of the car ahead of her. "You can just relax and chill with Jill."

Rosalie was going home to visit her very large, very noisy, very-involved-in-her-life family back east for the holidays. Usually, Jessica didn't envy her at all, but this year, a little noise and over-involvement might have been nice.

Instead, she'd focus on an incredibly relaxing girls' week away with her best friend and a lot of sunshine.

The perfect answer to the holidays.

Matt poured himself another cup of coffee as Zoe and Soph rolled out more cookie dough behind him. Tonight had gone well. He'd hoped having everyone celebrating one more of their town's traditions would bring some of the naysayers around. But apparently, people thought you could have both small-town charm and big-city movie shoots in the same place at the same time.

Logic told him otherwise.

He took a sip, glad he remembered to switch to decaf, and watched the girls decorate another cookie.

From the parlor, the soft strains of "Rudolph, the Red Nosed Reindeer" kept him smiling.

Sure, their kitchen wasn't the super homey, oak and panels of the smaller houses, but the lodge's service-style kitchen was what he'd grown up with. It was just as homey to him as painted roosters, teapots, or whatever decorative things people picked were to them.

"So do you think she'll be nice?" Sophie asked, interrupting his thoughts.

"Who?"

Sophie threw her hands in the air and added on an exasperated sigh for good measure.

"Jessica McEllis?" Matt was starting to worry a little about this obsession. "I don't know, sweetie. I think she will be."

Because what did you say to your ten-year-old daughter about the woman who it was quickly becoming obvious was her hero?

"Do you think she'll like me?"

"Sophie." Zoe flicked a bit of frosting at her, and Matt fought the urge to put a stop to the potential frosting fight. "That's a no-brainer. How could anyone not like you?"

"Hailey Shephard doesn't like me."

"Wait." Matt set his coffee down, surprised at this turn of events. "I thought she was your friend."

"That's the other Hailey." Apparently, their small town was filled with them. "Hailey Shephard does *not* like me."

What kind of idiot didn't love his daughter?

"Well, she should. You're smart, you're cool—"

"Dad!" Sophie shook her head.

Matt wasn't so old that he didn't remember that your parents' love didn't count.

"And," Zoe jumped in, bringing the conversation back around while handing Sophie a cookie for good measure, "I think Jessica's going to love you."

"I'm not supposed to eat sweets before bedtime." Sophie eyed the cookie as if it were the last one she'd ever get.

"Luckily, I know your father."

Sophie glanced his way with a desperation that bordered on pathetic.

Matt let her hang for a second before giving the nod, watching the two girls giggle over cookies while finishing the decorations.

He shared a look with Zoe over Soph's head as she bit into the angel's wing. He got that this was a big deal, but what were they going to do if these movie people were rude or mean?

The one hard thing about running Homestead Lodge was having strangers in their home every day. Typically, it didn't matter. People came and went. But now that Sophie was fixated on this actress, he wasn't sure how he'd handle it if she was hurt by her idol.

"Don't borrow worry." Zoe shoved an empty mixing bowl at him and motioned toward the sink.

"I'm not."

"I can all but feel it rolling off you. Sophie will be

fine." She joined him at the sink, setting the rinsed bowls in the dishwasher. "I'm betting we see very little of them. I'm sure two weeks isn't that long with such a big project. We're more likely to have to explain to Sophie that they're busy than make excuses for them being rude or dismissive."

"I just don't want to see her get hurt." She'd already lost too much.

Zoe patted his arm. "She's stronger than you think. And so are you."

Matt stood in the dim light of the kitchen as Zoe walked away down the hall, flicking off switches as she went, and wondered just how strong he'd need to be to get through another year of change.

The next morning at the lodge was quiet as they waited for their next round of guests to join them. The perfect time to get some errands done.

Matt finished his morning sweep of the grounds to make sure everything was in order then came in to find Zoe at the front desk, reviewing this week's schedule. He bit his tongue when he saw Sophie was watching yet another dragon movie. Maybe he'd ask Zoe more about them later. She typically had a pretty good idea about all things pop culture.

"I have to run over to the bakery to pick up the pumpkin pies. Soph, you want to come with me?" He watched her as she stared at the screen, completely oblivious to his question. Shaking his head, he glanced at Zoe. "Just a big ball of holiday spirit, isn't she?"

With a push toward the door, Zoe handed him his coat and sent him on his way. The girls were obviously Team Get Dad Out today, so Matt thought he'd enjoy the walk over instead of driving. The snow from the evening before had broken, leaving a clear sky and a shoveled sidewalk in its wake.

As he stepped outside, he took a deep breath. The air was just chilly enough to be a wake-up call. He knew the walk was the right decision as he headed downtown. The square was alive with people running errands and rushing around. Even the wintery temperature couldn't keep Homesteaders inside. One more thing he loved about them. The weather was the weather. Iowa was hot in the summer and cold in the winter, just as it was intended.

He'd gotten used to getting around town taking him even longer now that he was mayor. Everyone wanted to stop and comment on something or make a suggestion. He didn't mind. He actually loved that he wasn't expected to only be on duty when sitting behind a desk in a suit.

And that no one expected that of him, either.

If they had a problem, they knew where the lodge was and to just stop in. He'd give them a warm cup of coffee and a sympathetic ear to explain their issue.

It was how things were done. He couldn't imagine it any other way. Office hours, secretaries, and meetings for no reason just weren't the way here in Homestead.

Stomping his boots on the sidewalk outside the bakery, he pushed the door open and let himself be overtaken by the waft of sweetly-scented breads and desserts. Lucky for him, the shop was empty except for the owner and best pie baker in four counties.

"Merry Christmas, Pauline."

"Morning, Matt." She set aside the cookie tray she was arranging for display. "Here for your pies?"

"Yes, ma'am. It isn't Christmas without Pauline's famous pumpkin pies." He looked forward to them every year. Somewhere, in an alternate universe, pumpkin pies were in season year-round.

Maybe in one of those movies Sophie was obsessed with.

"Aren't you sweet. I've got them in the back." She stopped at the little swinging door that led to the kitchen where she made the magic. "Oh... and I have a little something extra for Sophie."

"*Pauline.*" He laughed. He couldn't go anywhere without someone wanting to spoil his daughter. "There's no need for that. You spoil her."

She waved him off with a "*pshaw*" before she pointed him toward the coffee pot behind the counter and hurried to the back. "Help yourself to some coffee."

"Thank you," he shouted to her retreating figure. Coffee was exactly what he needed.

Matt felt gratitude to the bottom of his soul. When he'd lost Melanie, the town had stepped in, helping him raise Sophie and hold it together. They'd become more than neighbors—they'd become family.

He took a deep sip of the coffee and breathed in the bakery goodness.

Maybe he'd let Sophie have whatever her special treat was when he got home instead of saving it for after dinner.

After all, Christmas only came once a year.

CHAPTER FIVE

Jessica sat back and glanced out the rented SUV's window as snow went by. And then more snow. And then *more* snow.

The drive from the airport had been longer than she'd expected. Who put airports that far away from things? In L.A., it might have taken this long to go four miles. She probably should have been watching the scenery rush past instead of working, but snow-covered trees all looked the same when Gavin was driving sixty-five miles an hour.

Finally, they slowed down, pulling into a low-speed area with a *Welcome to Homestead* sign announcing they'd arrived.

She set her script aside, taking in the entire look of the holiday embellishments.

"Look at all the Christmas stuff." She couldn't help but feel the adrenaline rush through her as she took stock of the town and how every corner overflowed with decorations. In her mind, she could see the movie shot by shot as they drove by the locations already set up for their storytelling to begin. "The crew has done a great job with the set decorations."

"The crew doesn't get here until tomorrow." Rosalie flashed her a bright smile as they watched the bright colors and twinkling lights slide by.

Jess glanced out the window again, taking in the beauty and perfection of every light, every ornament. She would never have thought something so detailed lived outside a sound stage.

"Wait, so all this is… The town did all this?"

"Yeah." Rosalie leaned past her to take in the same view. "They really like Christmas."

She could hear the happiness in Rosalie's voice. Suddenly, this year she was all about the holidays. Jess wouldn't be surprised if her typically straitlaced PR manager started dressing as an elf and delivering presents.

"Wow." Jess took another look out the window. This place was too much. Barbara wasn't kidding when she said these people loved the holidays.

And yet, it managed to not be too much. Instead of being hokey, tacky, or overdone, the decorations had a warmth that put her at ease immediately.

The shops were all decorated with themes for their clientele. A toy store with a Christmas train, a dress shop with holiday party dresses, a bakery with giant Christmas cookies in the window.

"Oh, hey! Gavin, pull over."

"What are you doing?" Rosalie glanced around as Jessica tossed her planner on the seat beside her.

"It's a bakery. I want to get something for the crew. Cupcakes! I'm going to be their favorite producer ever." She wasn't above blatant bribery from the very beginning. And, with cupcakes, they'd know it was a bribe, so it wasn't sneaky. It was just—smart. "I'll be right back."

Jess barely waited for Gavin to pull over. The inside of the bakery was as cute as the outside. And the smells. Lordy, she probably gained six pounds just walking through the door. There were cute little tables next to the door and rows of bread in oversized baskets off to her right. But in front of her was a colorful display of cookies, cakes, cupcakes, éclairs... all the things her trainer would put down as a hard no.

And to top it all off, the guy behind the counter was adorable.

She took a second glance, trying not to focus on him when she'd come in for cupcakes. This was work, not a chance to check out the hottie at the bakery.

She'd watched those reality shows with bakers. They had super-cut arms from all that baker stuff she didn't understand because... kitchens and Jessica had never been a match made in heaven.

This one was tall and lean, obviously not a body builder, but with a strength to him in the way he stood and crossed over behind the counter to meet her. The deep chocolate of his eyes pulled her in when she let her gaze come back up to his face. And scruff. Actual guy scruff. Not that well-manicured facial hair so many of her colleagues passed off. This was a man who got up with more important things to do this morning than shave.

There was something so incredibly attractive about that.

She shifted her gaze back to him again, trying to keep her smile professional.

"Hi." She felt herself blushing. "Can I get, like, a hundred cupcakes?"

One hundred would be more than enough—and she'd seen those guys eat. They worked hard all day, so a cupcake or two was no problem for their waistlines.

She focused on the cupcakes, trying to force the heat from her face.

It had been years since she'd blushed. Jess had thought she'd trained it out of herself, but there was something about this guy.

"Oh, I'm not—" The guy started, but Jess was afraid to let herself get sidetracked.

"Chocolate, vanilla, red velvet..." *Wait. That might be too fancy for small-town bakeries.* "Do they have red velvet in Iowa?"

"Oh." The baker guy set down his coffee. "You must be with the movie."

He gave her a look she couldn't read, but she figured the people up here wouldn't be used to dealing with celebrities.

"I am." Obviously, they were going to be a little

starstruck. She shouldn't have been surprised, but she'd just gotten here. "Do you want an autograph?"

"No, that's okay."

Even his voice, deep with a bit of gravel to it, wasn't the polished form of masculinity she'd been surrounded by for the last fifteen years.

For some reason, Jess knew she had to get out of there before she did something to embarrass herself.

"Oh, don't be shy." Jessica grabbed a napkin with the bakery's name on it while flashing him a smile and hoped her hands didn't shake while she signed it. He could frame it if it was on one with his logo. "Here. Don't sell that on eBay!"

"Why would I sell—?"

She set the napkin on the counter and started to back away, to find her center again as she figured out exactly what was going on with her.

"Great." She glanced around, knowing there was no use trying to talk someone out of doing something they already knew they were going to do. "So, the cupcakes?"

"You need to talk to—"

"Can they be ready on Monday?" She thought about the fact that this tiny bakery might not have the help for a rush job. "I'll pay extra. That would be amazing. Okay? Thanks! Bye!"

"But—"

"I'll send someone back for them." She gave him a wave. Cute or not, she wasn't here to get hit on by bakers—no matter how much she wished she could stay and flirt. She'd put in her order like a normal person and would let Rosalie deal with paying him.

That was actually kind of fun. It had been a long time since she'd gotten to run a normal errand on her own. Maybe this Iowa thing wouldn't be so bad after all.

And she still had Fiji with her friend Jill in less than two weeks.

A little bit of normal followed up by some resort relaxing.

"Jessica." *Oh no.* "Jessica! What's going on with you and Vince?"

"You've got to be kidding me." Jess stopped, sparing a moment to glare at Ian before glancing around for more paparazzi with cameras pointed at her. There went her happy cupcake buzz. She'd felt so normal in there. Just a girl ordering cupcakes from a guy who was super delicious-looking himself. "Where's the rest of the horde?"

"Just me so far." He sounded oddly proud. "How about an exclusive?"

She'd always tried to be nice and fair to these guys, but this was too much. She was a thousand miles from Hollywood, and they weren't even on production time yet.

"Sure." She glanced back to give Gavin the come-save-me sign. "You can have an exclusive, up-close look at my bodyguard."

Gavin stepped between them, his hand coming up toward the camera—the only thing that would get Ian, or any of them, to back off. She hated playing the threat card, but Gavin knew how to make things look more intimidating than they were. She had no idea how she'd navigate her world without him.

"All right, Gavin. Stand down." Ian raised his hands over his head in defeat with the camera pointing away. He turned enough to keep his attention on her. "Jessica, I'm just doing my job."

She shook her head, smiling at him sadly. "You have a lousy job, Ian."

"Tell me about it." He was already checking his camera.

She didn't give him the clearance to take photos he wanted as Gavin handed her back into the car. She'd enjoyed her time in the bakery, ordering cupcakes, of all things, not to mention the unfamiliar heat of a new guy. But then had to walk right back into La-La-Land-ness with paparazzi so quickly her head spun.

Letting her eyes drift shut, she let the worries that had rushed through her ease back out. One paparazzi did not mean she'd been overrun with them. She could manage Ian—or Gavin could.

Beside her, Rosalie was already making calls to ensure that her privacy was as intact as possible.

By the time they arrived at the Homestead Lodge, she'd calmed down. She was lucky she had a team like Rosalie and Gavin to support her. Both of them had been with her forever, and she knew her trust in them was always well-placed.

Gavin slowed and pulled into a short, circular drive that led up to a stunning white house with a wrap-around porch. It was lined with white lights and had beautiful wooden Adirondack chairs and a swing at one end.

It was exactly what she'd expect for a small-town inn—simply lovely.

Gavin pulled to the front door, letting the ladies out and then going back for the luggage.

As she followed Rosalie into the lodge, she couldn't help but take in the beautiful decorations, many looking like handcrafted artisan work. It was just as homey as she'd hoped, and she wondered why they hadn't gotten permission to do interior shots here. They were renting out the whole space for privacy, so it wasn't like they'd bother any other guests.

She glanced down the hall as Rosalie made her way over to the beautiful wooden reception desk in the first room. On the opposite side of the hall were sitting rooms and a dining room. It was all usable space, but she liked her privacy. She wandered in to see how much space there was in case they needed to work in there. Hopefully, her suite was spacious enough to have any meetings she needed to have with her team when not at her trailer.

"Hi. Checking in." Across the hall, Rosalie was taking charge and getting it done, just like always. "Two rooms under Evans and one for Williams."

"Yes. Everything is all set." A woman's voice followed. "Let me get your paperwork from the back."

Rosalie leaned into the front room to give Jess a quick nod to let her know it was under control.

It was a bit surreal when Jessica heard her own voice from the next room yelling, "Stand back!"

She peeked into one of the sitting rooms to see a girl about ten watching *Asterlight* on her iPad. Jess wandered in and sat down next to her, smiling to herself when the girl all but ignored her.

"What'cha watching?" Jessica wasn't used to seeing kids randomly sitting around enjoying her movies. But this one was adorable.

"*Asterlight: Dragon Wars*," she said, not giving Jess any of her attention.

"Is it any good?" Jessica knew the answer. *Dragon Wars* was her best-selling movie, the one that had made her a household name.

"It's not the best one."

Wait, what?

"It's not?" She'd gotten more nominations from this movie than any other. It had made her career. It was the first movie mentioned in any bio about her anywhere.

"*The Dark Forest* is better. But my all-time favorite is—" The girl finally looked away from the screen and stuttered to a stop. Jessica loved the moments she met fans—real fans.

This girl obviously was a lover of the movies if she could compare them all. Not to mention she was sitting here watching one of the older ones.

So when she jumped up and started shouting, "Oh, man! Oh, wow. Oh, man!", it more than made Jessica's day.

"Hi, I'm Jessica." She gave the girl a smile, thrilled to be off to great a start in Homestead. "What's your name?"

"Sophie Larson!" she shouted before rushing on, her excitement almost blending into one big word. "I've seen all your movies. Well, not all of them. Dad wouldn't let me see *The Heavy Heart* because of the kissing, but I've seen the *Asterlight* movies a billion times."

"A billion? That's a lot."

It never failed to floor her when someone loved her movies this much. People didn't typically appreciate all the work that went into movies, so when a fan really loved the outcome, it made it all worth it.

"I can't believe it's really you!" Sophie was looking at her like she was the superhero, not just the actress.

"I can't believe it sometimes, either," Jessica whispered and glanced around, really letting that sink in. It had been years since being her had been novel. But with this new role and being on the production side, it was like she was seeing everything anew. "So, are you staying here?"

"No, I live here." Sophie nodded her head toward the far side of the inn. "On the other side of the lodge."

"Do your parents own the lodge?" Because if Sophie loved her movies, hopefully, she had more fans running the lodge... and the town. It would definitely make things easier. Especially with some of the Homestead officials not thrilled.

"My dad and aunt do."

Before Jessica could respond, the sound of the front door falling shut echoed down the hall.

"Dad!" Sophie shouted. "Look! It's Jessica McEllis."

Jessica turned to find the cute baker standing in the doorway, carrying a couple of pies.

Oh, no.

Of all the inns in all the world, he had to walk into this one.

The same butterflies that had attacked her stomach at the bakery started fluttering again.

"Ohhhh. Okay..." He came into the room, giving Jessica what was obviously his polite smile. "The autograph makes more sense now."

"Wait— You got her autograph?" Sophie rushed toward him, hand out, obviously assuming that whatever autograph he was carrying was now hers. "Where is it? I want to see it."

"Ummm..." Matt glanced between her and his daughter, perhaps not wanting to say he'd tossed the autograph in the trash.

She stood, desperately trying to find words to apologize.

"So you don't work at the bakery?" Because why not just get all the embarrassment out of the way in one swoop?

"No. I was just there to pick up some pies..." He nodded down to the pies in his hands. Guess there wasn't door-to-door pie delivery. Which would have been much better. Much less embarrassing. He went on, in case he wasn't being clear enough. "... for the lodge."

"That you own." *Oh geez.* Jessica didn't think this could get more awkward. And that meant she'd basically went in there, gone all famous-person on him, demanded cupcakes, given him an unwanted autograph, and swept out.

Jessica could feel her face burning. Talk about cliché.

While she'd been thinking how hot he was, he'd probably been thinking that she was a major prima donna.

"Got it." She forced a smile, which was calling up every acting bone she had in her body. "Sorry."

"I didn't realize who you were, either, so we're even." He didn't sound too sure about that, but he held his hand out anyway. "I'm Matt."

When she took his hand, a shock washed over her. She glanced up to catch the look on his face, wondering if he'd felt it, too.

This guy was too—real. She couldn't seem to stop herself from pausing and looking into his dark brown eyes. They crinkled at the corners. So many of her costars were now on the botox bus that it was nice to see a guy who had laugh lines.

Her gaze swept the room, recognizing—maybe for the first time—that Homestead wasn't a set. It wasn't just a location. The lodge was these people's home.

Trying to figure out how to extricate herself from the situation was almost as embarrassing as that time at the Emmys when she called Denzel "Dezi" because she was so nervous she couldn't get his whole name out.

In her defense, it was *Denzel,* and she'd challenge any woman to stay grounded in the sphere of his looks and charm.

At that moment, an adorable girl in her late twenties, who looked so much like him that she could only be Matt's sister, rushed in.

"And that's my sister, Zoe." Matt nodded toward the young woman where she'd frozen. Then he pointed at the girl she'd just been sitting with. "And this is my daughter, Sophie."

"Hey, Zoe." Jessica smiled and waited—the long, awkward wait that happened so often while people processed they were meeting someone famous. When Zoe didn't have anything to add to her wave, she turned back to the girl, flashing her a smile. "Sophie."

Rosalie joined them and Jess was thrilled to have someone on her team back in the game. As always, Rosalie broke the silence.

"Hi." She crossed to where Jessica stood between Matt and Sophie, doing her quick social math and seeing that things were not all easy-peasy in the room. "I'm Jessica's publicist, Rosalie, and this is Gavin."

Matt's natural hospitality and business sense must have kicked in, because he swept a smile across the entire group, much warmer than when he'd spotted her in his parlor. "Welcome to the Homestead Lodge."

"Thank you." Jess glanced around, glad to be able to say something completely honest and heartfelt. "It's really beautiful."

"Thank you. I appreciate that. We take a lot of

pride in it." He obviously meant that sincerely even though he was giving her his owner-of-the-inn smile. Jess tried not to feel disappointed as he passed her on to his sister. "So, Zoe has your room keys. Please just let us know if you need anything."

Obviously, he wanted to end the awkwardness as badly as she did.

Or just escape the prima donna who kept staring at him.

Jess gave Rosalie a nod no one else would have noticed and let her take over the arrangements. While Rosalie dealt with a still-stunned Zoe, Jessica knew she needed to make one more go at making things comfortable between her and the handsome inn guy, formerly—and incorrectly—the handsome baker guy.

She stepped into her comfort zone: playing a part.

The role she picked was the cute actress out of her element who needed help.

"Actually, could you help me get in contact with the town's mayor?" She leaned in, giving him the grin that had gotten her the part of Romea in the role-reversal Romeo and Juliet the director had initially said she was too popular to pull off. "I've heard he's a bit of a stick-in-the-mud and doesn't want us Hollywood types ruining Christmas."

Sophie chimed in when Matt didn't answer immediately. "Dad… is the mayor."

Of course he was.

Jessica considered telling Gavin to put all the

trunks back in the car and heading back to the airport right then.

"You're the…"

"Stick-in-the-mud." He gave a brief wave with his free hand. "Yeah. Hi."

"Oh. Yeah. Wow." Jess shook her head, trying to figure out what to say to that. "I am so sorry."

Great.

Serously. She should put everything she'd brought with her right back in the car. *Variety* wouldn't make too big a deal about it in their next issue, right? If they didn't, there was always *TMZ*. And, she couldn't forget, Paparazzi Ian was already walking the streets of Homestead.

"Why don't we set up time for you two to talk tomorrow?" Rosalie pulled out her ever-present planner and looked through the openings for the next day. "Maybe you can give us a tour of the town? Ten a.m.?"

"Sure." Matt's attention drifted back to her from Rosalie, surprising her that he'd bother. "We can do that."

Jessica answered before Rosalie could. "Thank you. Listen, we are not going to be in your way. We don't want to change a thing. You won't even know we're here."

He gave her another tight smile, obviously not expecting to see any of that happen. Before she could say anything else, he turned and carried his pies out of the room.

Zoe and Sophie stood together at the doorway, smiling at her half apologetically, half still starstruck.

"He'll get over it." Zoe shrugged. "He's just very protective of the town."

Great. They'd found the only town in America with a mayor who actually wanted to take care of his people.

With that, Rosalie laid a hand on her back and steered her toward the stairs, extricating her from trying to come up with more ways to apologize.

Or embarrass herself.

Jessica took a deep breath, knowing she'd have to start fresh in the morning—in more ways than one.

Chapter Six

M att rolled over, trying not to growl like a bear as he glanced at the clock, not thrilled to see it say only 4:32 a.m.

That was early—even for innkeeper time.

What in the world had woken him up? He listened, afraid Sophie was up or having a bad dream.

Then he heard it, a low rumble and roar. The front of the house shook, enough to make him wonder what was going on, but not enough to worry something was wrong. At first, he thought it was a cold, hard nor'easter blowing in. But the rumbling just continued.

He threw on a bathrobe and hurried out the side entrance he and the girls used to get to their quarters.

Out front, rolling down Main Street one after another, huge trucks trundled past, not slowing for the town center or even the stop sign at the corner. At one point, one tooted his over-loud horn and kept moving.

"Yup, I don't even know they're here."

Sophie couldn't sleep.

Especially since Dad said she could go on the tour of the town with them today.

How could she sleep with her hero in the house? Jessica McEllis was here. Hailey Shephard would *never* top that—and it was totally okay if she hated Sophie more for this. Having Jessica here would be worth it.

She was sitting in the front room waiting for all the grownups to get their acts together when she heard someone coming down the front stairs.

Rushing out to the hall, she spotted Jessica's bodyguard, Gavin.

That's what she needed. A bodyguard. Imagine how jealous Hailey Shephard would be if she had Gavin taking care of it when she teased Sophie.

"Hi, Gavin!"

Gavin glanced down at the small person in front of him, looking confused, but Sophie knew she'd win him over.

"Hello."

"You're Jessica's bodyguard, right?" When Gavin nodded, she rushed on with her idea. "I think I should get a bodyguard. I mean, it's not like I have crazy fans, but I bet it would make Hailey Shephard jealous. She thinks she's special because she has a horse. But I'd be all, 'Big deal, I have a bodyguard.'"

Gavin glanced around the room, probably looking for Jessica. Sophie bet he was really good at his job, and that would be a definite plus if she could make him work for her.

"Have a seat." Sophie motioned to the stairs where she often sat with her dad when he got home.

Gavin plopped down on the fourth stair—one higher than her dad's because he was really tall.

"Not all the time," she rushed on. He'd looked really nervous for a moment there. Probably afraid he'd be letting Jessica down. "Just like for school and when I go to my piano lessons. Do you think Jessica would mind if I borrowed you?"

"Ummmm..."

Gavin glanced at his watch.

"Don't worry. You're early. We aren't going on our tour for another ten minutes."

"Oh."

"So, I was thinking about this because of the *Asterlight* movies—"

Sophie was lucky she had a plan. As soon as she explained it to Gavin, she knew he'd agree to be her bodyguard—even if it was just while they were here for the movie.

Jessica glanced in the mirror again. She needed to look perfect, but not too stylish. Maybe a little less city. Just, blend a bit. Less Hollywood for sure.

Not that she was trying to impress Matt. She was just aiming to be a professional.

She pretty much had decided she nailed it with a pair of slacks and a casual sweater. She reached for the sunglasses she typically hid behind, then thought better of it. After a last look, she was hoping for the best when there was a knock on the door.

"Come in."

Rosalie hurried in, full of purpose and plans, and gave her the once-over.

"Are you ready?" she asked, probably running through memorized schedules in her head.

"Almost." Jessica gave her reflection one more check. "How do I look?"

Rosalie glanced up, then back down at her files. "Fine."

"I mean..." Jessica ran a hand down the front of her sweater. "Do I look, you know, Iowa?"

She finally had Rosalie's attention. Her PR manager scanned her again before shaking her head.

"What are you talking about?" Rosalie asked.

"I don't want to be too Hollywood." This town was giving her something special. She wanted to make an effort. And she needed to win over the not old, not grumpy-looking (but still maybe a little grumpy) town mayor. "I want to fit in."

"Sweetie, you're a movie star, and he's the mayor of a small Midwest town."

She could all but hear Rosalie add, *and it's a meeting,* to the end of her sentence.

Jess knew that. It was just a very, very important meeting.

"I need to make up for the whole stick-in-the-mud thing." She checked out her reflection again. This was why she was an actress. She'd had no idea how much distance it had given her from making these social gaffes that she seemed to walk herself into constantly. "I should have written notes. Can we call the writer? Have him whip up some stuff for me to say?"

"Jessica, relax! We'll '*ooh*' and '*ahh*,' you'll turn on your million-watt smile, and by the end of the tour, you'll have him eating out of your hand."

Rosalie ushered her through the door without giving her another moment to worry or argue.

Jess wasn't sure her million-watt anything would win Matt Larson over, but she figured she'd done enough damage already. How much worse could she make it?

Before Jessica reached the bottom of the stairs, she already heard Sophie talking to someone about the *Asterlight* series. She couldn't help but grin. One's biggest fans always made things better.

"So then last Christmas, I got the *Asterlight Chronicles* books," Sophie went on. "Like the whole set of real books, which is so cool. And I read them all, but I think the movies are better."

Jessica swung into the lobby, Rosalie on her heels, to find Gavin, standing at attention with her tiny fan next to him, talking his ear off.

She'd seen Gavin run off paparazzi, handle intrusive fans, brush by reporters, and even take down a stalker, but she'd never seen him like this.

Gavin had met his match.

This was what out-of-your-comfort-zone looked like on a nerves-of-steel superhero.

And his match liked her movies better than the books.

Jessica stepped into the foyer to join them, pulling Sophie's attention off her new compatriot. "So do I."

As soon as she spoke, Sophie was at her side. "Good morning!"

"Morning, Sophie." At least someone was happy to see her.

"Dad said I could go on the tour as long as I don't bug you."

Jessica suspected her presence was more to make sure her dad didn't have to do all the talking. But since she was thrilled to have the girl along with them, it was all good.

"You could never bug me." As soon as the words slipped out, she suspected they were true. She really did enjoy Sophie's company.

Enter the annoyed mayor, stage... wherever their innkeeper quarters were. And, boy did he look even less happy to see her than when he'd wandered off last night.

"Morning."

"Good morning." Jessica shot him a smile as Sophie's grin bounced between them, practically lighting up what would have been an otherwise gloomy morning meeting.

"So, are we ready for the tour?" Matt slid his jacket

on, glancing around the collection of people in his foyer, his gaze pausing on Jess for a long heartbeat of a moment.

"Absolutely. I can't wait." Jessica wasn't lying. The town was adorable. It was her stage set come to life. And the people must be just as great if Matt was willing to go to lengths to protect them.

"Great." Matt was a professional in the hospitality arena, not to mention the mayorship, and the tour was going to happen whether he wished he could run her whole crew out of town or not. "Let's get started."

Jessica leaned into Rosalie. "I can't imagine how this could be any more awkward."

Rosalie gave her a look, and the two women pulled on their jackets.

"Hey," Vince's voice called to them as he came down the hall.

"Oh, no."

"Where's everybody off to?" Vince asked, dropping a heavy hand on Matt's shoulder.

Jessica looked at Rosalie and read the same panic in her face.

This was not going to end well.

As Matt showed them around, Jessica plastered a smile on her face, making sure she gave every person they passed a nod. She got just enough attention that it was obvious they knew who she was, but not so much that it slowed them down. It was interesting.

At first, she thought it was Gavin, but then she caught on that Matt was giving anyone who might have approached a look that clearly said this was work and to wait till later.

The tour was really driving home that she was a guest in his town. They obviously liked and respected him.

With that in mind, she knew she was going to have to try harder to smooth the way. She'd have to win him over to make this shoot a success.

Easier said than done.

"And over there is the Homestead Cafe." Matt was giving them the two-cent tour as he sped them by the storefront.

"They have the best hamburgers." At least Sophie was enjoying the outing. She had something to add about the awesomeness of every business, shop, and event her dad mentioned.

The least Jessica could do was share her enthusiasm. "Who doesn't love a good burger?"

"You don't." Vince pushed his way to the front of the group. "You hate hamburgers."

"No, I don't."

"Yes. You do," Vince went on, laughing at her denial. "Remember when we took the jet to Martha's Vineyard for the weekend and stopped at that little diner—"

"So, Matt," Rosalie jumped in, trying to divert Vince's walk down memory lane. Thank goodness Homestead's main street was only so long. "Did you grow up here?"

"Born and raised," he said with a quiet pride that pulled Jessica's attention back to him.

"And the lodge?" Jess asked.

"It was my parents' place." He smiled. It was obvious from the way his voice changed how important they were to him. "They retired to Florida, so my sister and I took it over."

"That's nice." She meant it. It was nice. More than nice. The idea of something so solid being passed from one generation to another had a deep, grounding feel to it. "Keeping the business in the family."

She felt Vince pushing his way to her side again before she heard him jump in.

"Jess and I stayed at this amazing inn when we were in Budapest," Vince interrupted. "Honey, remember that? It was like a castle—"

"And so," Jessica jumped in, talking over Vince—because, what in the world was going on with him? "You're the mayor, as well. Impressive. You must really love it here."

"I do," Matt answered as he waved to someone shouting a good morning greeting to him.

"Well, I can see why." There actually was a lot of beauty in it. "It's got that great small-town charm—"

"Make way!" A guy with a dolly filled with props crossed the street as they turned the corner and ran straight into backstage Grand Central Station. It was filled with production trailers, dressing rooms, lights, and basically everything you'd need to make a movie.

The noise was incrementally worse the farther

they walked. Machinery setting up cameras and mics, the trackway being laid, everything was adding to the noise as they dodged another set designer rushing by.

"Yeah." Matt glowered at the ruckus. "Nice and quiet here."

Everyone in the group fell silent as they kept walking.

Jessica didn't know what to say to try to make it better. She just knew she had to.

CHAPTER SEVEN

I an Carter was not loving his job.

He kind of wondered if he'd ever loved it. The idea of being a Hollywood photographer had seemed so glamorous at first. Taking photos of some of the most beautiful people in the world—actors, models, athletes. Basically, anyone who was a celebrity was on the "get" list.

What he had really wanted to do was portrait shots. Not like Leibovitz. His thing, the idea he wanted to share, was that these celebrities were people under it all. Sure, they might be more beautiful, more talented, and richer than the rest of us, but they were still people.

Casual shots that showed you who the celebrity really was would be great. Doing something they loved, or maybe at home.

So, how he found himself nowhere near Jessica McEllis's home following her around a small town in Iowa was beyond him.

Oh, yeah. He needed to pay his bills.

But the sad thing about being paparazzi was the pay promised to be substantial—one more picture, one snap of just the right moment, and a guy could retire for life and take photos of what he wanted.

He glared down at his phone as it gave a shrill ring, knowing he didn't really have a choice but to answer it since he was here on someone else's dime. But Jessica had nailed it earlier—sometimes his job was lousy.

Of course, it could be awesome, too. He wasn't a martyr. But he wasn't a great guy, either. Not exactly something anyone wanted to admit to himself, but what else could he say when he stood staring up at the window of a young woman's room at an inn, wondering how to get pictures from the outside?

"How's it going? You gonna have anything good to send me?" Mickey, the guy who was currently The Boss of Ian, asked.

"I'm freezing, Mickey. That's how it's going." Ian looked at all the snow he was standing in and suddenly understood why Mickey had offered to pay his way to Jessica's current location shoot for a larger cut of the pictures. "Yeah, I got a few of Jessica and some of Vince but nothing interesting."

"I didn't send you up there to get shots of them working." Mickey huffed out a breath. "Get me something good."

Ian bit his tongue instead of asking Mickey how he expected him to do that. The guy probably wasn't above doing whatever it took to get a picture that told a story he wanted—*any* story he wanted.

"Yeah, yeah. I got it, and trust me, you'll be the first to know."

Because as soon as he shot something worth selling, he was out of here. He hit the END button and glanced up at the second floor again.

This was so not going to be fun.

He wrapped his camera around his neck and tucked it inside his jacket, praying nothing would happen to his baby on this death mission. Approaching the tree, he wondered why kids were so interested in doing this. It seemed pretty risky just to get a couple feet off the ground.

Then again, he had young nephews—they seemed to bounce.

When had he stopped bouncing?

He climbed up on a stone wall that the thick trunk of the tree leaned against and hauled himself onto the first branch. From there, it was easier to get himself high enough. Once he'd settled into a thick V of branches outside Jessica's room, he settled in to get some preliminary shots. His stomach turned as he remembered the argument about crossing lines he'd had with Mickey.

He had lines, darn it.

Of course, he wouldn't take anything risqué. He liked Jessica. He wouldn't do that to her. He wouldn't do that to *anyone*, really, but especially someone like her.

She was nice to them even when it was obvious she just wanted to be left alone.

Focusing his lens, he took in the view. It was a great room. Not the plush surroundings he was used to shooting her in, but homey. He could work with this. It actually might let him do a softer-side type thing.

"Hey!" someone shouted from beneath him. "What are you doing?"

Ian jumped and reached out for a branch to steady himself but missed, falling right past it... and into a huge pile of snow.

Snow—it was as cold as he thought it would be.

"Oh my gosh!" The woman who had shouted at him rushed over to make sure he wasn't dead.

In this small of a town, maybe they'd just bury the body and be good with it.

Come to think of it, a lot of horror movies happened in small towns.

Ian shoved that thought to the back of his mind as snow turned to water and ran down his back. He let the shock of it bring him around to his senses but pulled himself out of the pile at the idea that his equipment might be getting wet.

"Are you okay?" The girl stood over him, all flushed cheeks and bouncing, short curls.

"I'm..." He looked at her again. "I'm..."

"You know what?" she asked, as if he'd have a clue. "We should get you inside and check your head."

Ian nodded and let her help him up. Obviously,

he wasn't thinking straight. He was on the job, but instead of focusing on how to get another shot at that room, he was letting the adorable girl lead him into the kitchen attached to the lodge. Before he knew it, he was pushed into a chair and had a bag of ice propped on the knee he'd landed on.

Of course, he could justify this by claiming to be getting a lay of the land.

"So, are you like… a paparazzi?" She seemed suspicious now that she knew he hadn't died.

"Paparazzo. Paparazzi is plural." Because semantics was really going to help this situation.

"Oh," she said almost innocently. "So, a bunch of vulture photographers is paparazzi, and one vulture climbing a tree in my backyard is a paparazzo?"

Ian let his head drop against the wall behind him.

"How can you do that?" she asked as she sat next to him, obviously studying him like he was some sort of exotic fungus. "Chase famous people around and invade their privacy?"

Ian shook his head. She made it sound like he had an option.

"We all have jobs to do." Ian gave her a look, assuming she was just another person like him, trying to make ends meet. Of course, Hollywood "ends meet" was crazy, but still. "What's yours? Are you a maid here or…?"

She straightened, her annoyance so clear he knew he'd made the wrong step right away.

"My brother and I own the place." She gave him

another look, obviously incredibly unimpressed with him. "And it's called housekeeping."

Great. One of the owners had caught him peeking in their second-floor window. He strongly doubted that a small town like Homestead saw this the same way L.A. did. In L.A., you'd get a slap on the wrist. Here, you'd probably end up doing hard manual labor.

Someone had to shovel those sidewalks clean, right?

"Aren't you a little young to be a business owner?"

She glared. He was obviously not winning any points. Didn't all women like to be told they looked young?

"I intend to have a chain of these lodges around the country by the time I'm thirty." Obviously, ambition wasn't a problem for her. "Aren't you a little old to be climbing trees?"

"Touché." That was enough of that. Ian knew when he'd worn out his welcome, but it typically didn't—Wait. Yes, it did happen that quickly all the time. His job was not exactly the most friend-centric one. Maybe he should start telling people he was an accountant. "Well, I better get going. No rest for the wicked and all that."

"Just a warning: if I see you back here again, I will call the sheriff." She crossed her arms, looking way tougher than he'd expected.

He didn't doubt she was serious. He'd learned this town and its population were very tight. He imagined they looked out for their guests just as strongly.

"Wouldn't be the first time." Ian handed her the ice, wishing the look she gave him as he left wasn't just as chilly. "Thanks for the ice pack…"

"Zoe."

"Zoe." Great name; it fit her. "Ian Carter, Vulture."

With a tip of his hat—well, the hat he'd be wearing if his head wasn't covered with this snow-guard of a wool cap—he headed out the door, pulling it shut behind him.

It felt like he'd been closing too many darn doors lately.

Glancing over his shoulder, he brushed it off. Like he'd told Zoe, no rest for the wicked.

Matt wasn't sure how this tour had turned bad.

Okay, so it hadn't started great, but the level of discomfort seemed to rise every time he tried to bring it back down.

Of course, he hadn't been thrilled to be sucked into the Hollywood introduction to Homestead. But he was the mayor and they were staying at his lodge.

Now, he had no problems with Sophie wanting to go on the tour he had been cornered into. It wasn't so much the awkward misunderstanding of who Jessica was or who he was. It was more that gut punch he'd felt when he'd seen her in the bakery that the first time.

He'd turned around and his heart had literally

stopped beating for a moment. He wasn't sure he'd taken a breath for a full minute. She'd stood there, smiling and looking around the bakery like she'd never been in one before, and he'd thought she brought the sunshine.

He hadn't had a moment like that since Melanie, and he hadn't expected to have one ever again.

And then she'd opened her mouth, assumed he worked at the bakery, tossed out an order, presumed they didn't know what red velvet was, and breezed out.

He'd almost managed to shake off the shock of it when he'd walked into his own home and found her standing there with his daughter, looking like she belonged.

In that split second, he'd nearly talked himself out of everything he believed in for a smile from her. And then she'd reminded him of who she was—of who *he* was—with the crack about the stick-in-the-mud mayor.

So now, here he was with her and her entourage, giving a tour of Homestead at high speed because he seriously doubted any of them actually cared about it.

And each time he managed to relax, to start to enjoy showing his town to outsiders in an attempt to win them over, Mr. Action Star would jump in and talk about dinner at the top of the Eiffel Tower or whatever other rich, famous-person adventure they'd gone on.

But it was good. He told himself again to just focus

on his job and let the attraction he felt every time he looked at her ride itself out.

She was a Hollywood somebody, and he was a guy who lived and breathed for his family and this small town.

Of course, she wouldn't be interested, and even if she were, talk about a bad match.

He waved at Mrs. Ingles from the grocery as he steered Sophie around a fire hydrant, her ongoing narration of the town and the best parts—as seen by a ten-year-old—keeping the group at a more comfortable pace.

So when he looked back up and saw Jessica smiling at her as they turned the corner, he shook it off and kept thinking about how to keep Homestead's traditions safe instead of that new flash of sunshine.

Jessica was a desperate woman.

Well, more desperate.

As they walked through town, equipment kept popping up, getting in the way, and making really awkward, loud noises.

No matter what she did to try to distract him, Matt couldn't seem to focus past the organized chaos happening on his main street. Of course, he probably didn't see the organized part of "organized chaos."

"So, Matt, how did all the Christmas festivities begin?" Nice, Jessica. Get him talking, thinking about things he loves. You'll just have to— "Watch your head!"

Matt ducked, grabbing Sophie as he did to make sure she wasn't anywhere near danger.

"Dad." She shook him off, her gaze taking in all the movie crew excitement. "You said you wouldn't embarrass me in front of the movie people."

Matt's gaze rolled toward heaven, and Jess could all but hear him whispering some ancient parental prayer.

"We've celebrated like this forever." He glanced around, probably feeling the history of his place here. She envied him that as he continued, "Since before I was born."

"We have the best Christmases of anyone." Sophie was obviously all-in on the holiday spirit, too. "There's a big tree, and carriage rides, and the snowman competition is tonight!"

"And it all culminates in the Festival of Lights on Christmas Eve." Matt grinned down at his daughter before shifting that smile to Jessica to pull her into their circle. "The entire town gets covered with Christmas lights."

He stopped short, pulling Sophie out of the way of a gaffer rushing by with equipment again.

"Hey, you gotta watch out around here, Soph. Okay?"

Vince leaned forward to stick his head between them. "They don't have Christmas lights in Fiji. There was one year when Jess and I were down at the beach. It was great, just us wearing our bathing suits and—"

Ok, that was it. Enough was enough.

"Hey, Vince, can I talk to you for a second?"

Without waiting for an answer, she took his arm and pulled him aside, glancing back to the flabbergasted group as she did. "Excuse us."

When they were just out of earshot, Vince grinned down at her, Mr. Innocent Guy smile firmly painted on his lips. If she hadn't known him for years, she might really believe the whole thing.

"What are you doing?" she asked.

"What do you mean?"

Vince was not a dumb guy. He might play the part in some of his macho action films, but he had brains to go with the brawn, and he was messing with one of the few people who truly knew that.

"What is with this walk down memory lane all of the sudden?"

Vince had never been the nostalgic type, even when they were together. She knew Rosalie had had to remind his assistant to remember their anniversary.

He wasn't a bad guy... he was just the stereotype of every guy rom-coms used to have a character arc.

"I don't know." He shrugged, giving her a look that bordered on sheepish. "Maybe it's the holidays. They make me nostalgic."

"Well, cut it out." How was he not seeing he was messing everything up? "I'm trying to get this guy to like me."

"You want him to *like* you?" Vince sounded as annoyed as he was surprised.

She tried not to blush at the idea. Matt totally wasn't her type. Beyond the whole grumpy-mayor thing, he was a small-town-loving, family-business-running dad who appreciated his life here… far, far away from anything Hollywood.

They couldn't be more different.

"Come on. Not like that," she insisted. "I'm trying to convince him that we aren't stuck-up movie stars, and your stories about us traipsing around the globe aren't helping. We need to find common ground."

There was no way Matt would trust his small town to her with the attitude Vince was flashing while speaking for both of them. And, on top of that, she was basically here to shoot a film about Matt's world—he must think they were nuts… or idiots.

"Oh! Why didn't you tell me?" Vince flashed her a smile that was obviously meant to relieve her—or someone who didn't know him as well. "I got this. I got you. No problem."

She wasn't worried… not even a little. Vince was a grown-up. She was sure he'd be totally professional about this now that he understood the stakes.

He turned and shouted back to where the group was.

"Hey, Matt. You know, I'm playing an innkeeper in this movie. Just like you!" He glanced toward Jessica and continued. He waved his hand between them, basically trying to show how similar they were—after all his talk about Fiji beaches and Budapest castles. Then, he quietly leaned back down to Jessica and asked, "How's that for common ground?"

Yeah. Totally great and subtle. Jessica rolled her eyes and kept going.

They turned the corner and came to a halt when they all but crashed into the action in the town square. Practically every inch of the formerly charming square was covered with equipment or people. It definitely did not have the quaint magic she'd seen when she'd arrived. It looked like every other back lot at this point.

She couldn't imagine how it appeared through Matt's eyes.

"I know this looks like a lot, but I promise once we get everything all set up, it'll be less intrusive."

She threw up a silent prayer that she wasn't accidentally lying. She went home at the end of the day on a shoot. Not this time... not here.

"Okay, good. Good. Well, this is the town square where we have our tree and our Santa..." Matt's voice faded off as he glanced around.

Sophie leaned on him, taking his hand. "Where's Santa?"

"Where's the tree?" Matt's tone echoed Sophie's.

Jessica looked around, desperately hoping she could point to the absent Christmas decorations.

"We had to strike them." Barbara strode up to join the group when she spotted them on the set. "They didn't work for us."

Sophie gasped, displeasure written all over her face. "They struck Santa?"

"Oh, sweetie, no." Jess tried not to glare at Barbara. Shouldn't she know better than to say stuff like that in front of a little girl? "It just means they took him down for a little while."

Sophie obviously was accepting Jessica's word, even though she didn't seem as relieved as Jessica had hoped.

"Everyone, this is Barbara McKeevers. She's our director."

The introductions weren't done—heck, they weren't really even started—when Matt jumped in.

"What's going on?"

"Oh, don't worry." Barbara waved him off, using her typical director speed and dismissive tone as she explained. "We'll put them back when we're done."

Before anyone could ask exactly when that would be, her phone buzzed.

"Excuse me." Barbara reached for it, answering it in one swift motion. "Hello? Sarah? Give your brother back his turtle."

Matt watched her go, obviously not thinking that was a good enough answer.

Jessica ran through every idea she could come up with, trying to think of a way to make this okay. She suspected that having the tree up only the day of Christmas Eve wasn't exactly how they enjoyed the holidays here.

"Jessica! Vince!" Oh, great. Just what she needed: Ian. "Any truth to the rumors that you're getting back together?"

Vince was no help at all. He gave Ian his aww-shucks grin and half-heartedly waved him off.

Matt turned his glare toward the photog as Gavin stepped between Ian and the group, leaving Rosalie to usher them all off like little ducks.

Just as she thought things couldn't get worse, the crew hauled Santa into the air and swung him over the roof of the bandstand. Sophie turned just in time to see it. With a gasp, she pointed up, turning everyone's attention to the character in flight.

Matt wrapped his arm around her and gave her a squeeze. "Santa's gonna be all right, sweetie."

But Santa was only supposed to fly with his reindeer.

CHAPTER EIGHT

The evening was quiet at the lodge. Matt wasn't used to so much midweek silence, but with the whole building rented out to the cast, it was empty when they were on set.

He should have been enjoying the quiet that evening, but he just kept coming back to the afternoon. They had a soft instrumental Christmas CD playing while Norah, the housekeeper reset the tables around them for the next day's breakfast.

Zoe sat next to him, going over menus and making adjustments for the holidays and their guests. She didn't seem upset by anything, but she'd always been a fly-by-the-seat-of-her-pants girl. This was probably just the excitement she needed.

He tried not to focus on other parts of the afternoon.

Parts with the dark-eyed actress with the bright smile.

But...

"Do you think Jessica and Vince Hawkins are getting back together again?"

Not that it mattered or anything. He was just… curious. They were living in his house, so to speak. And Sophie obviously hero-worshipped the ground Jessica walked on.

He wanted to make sure his daughter wasn't going to be getting the wrong idea about anything from her.

Zoe gave him a quick smile, glancing up from her work for a moment. "No. Why?"

"Nothing." Matt waved it off. "It's just something this photographer said."

The fact that he was asking about Hollywood gossip based on something a photographer had said while sitting in the kitchen with his sister was… mind-blowing.

What was his world coming to?

He glanced up when he realized Zoe hadn't said anything. She was just giving him a weird little look.

"Sorry." He let out a deep, frustrated sigh. Nothing about this situation made it easier to manage. The town and all its traditions were being sidelined or shifted for this movie. "That's not what I was thinking. I was thinking that she can't come in here and take over the town. I don't care how famous she is."

"Being famous can't be easy." Zoe's gaze drifted off as if picturing the difficulties of fame and fortune.

"Yeah." He could hear the bitterness in his voice but couldn't seem to stop himself. "I'm sure the mansions and the private jets must be quite tiring."

"But there's also the constant spotlight, people climbing trees to get a picture of you—"

"Climbing trees?" His sister always did have an imagination.

"I'm just saying," Zoe went on, "that underneath all that movie-star stuff is a person."

"You're right." Because what was he going to say? "You're absolutely right."

Zoe obviously didn't believe he was caving, but that wasn't what mattered right then.

"Well, I'm not going to let it bother me." He kept going when Zoe gave him a look. "Tonight's the snowman competition. We're going to win this year."

"Yeah, sure." Zoe laughed so hard she snorted. "Because our snowman doesn't end up looking more like a snow blob every year."

Matt was a big enough man to ignore the truth in this statement. "No, it doesn't!"

Zoe gave him a look and he shrugged. Sure. Maybe their yearly entry looked like a blob, but it was their blob—no, theirs and Sophie's. Another year of losing as a family just meant they were sticking to one more tradition.

And as he watched traditions fall around him, he hoped this was the blobbiest blob they'd ever made.

In her trailer, Jessica was going over her notes for the script again. Something had been bothering her since she'd signed off on the latest round of changes. It wasn't until she was here, on set, ready to shoot that it dawned on her what it might be.

Now, she glanced up from the script, second guessing her second guess.

"Do you think the kiss scene works?" she asked.

On the other side of her trailer's table, Rosalie shuffled through all the paperwork she was always managing.

"What do you mean?"

Jess shook her head, trying to put her thoughts into words.

"It's like it only happens because she's nostalgic for the kind of Christmas she had as a kid."

Now that she was here, in Homestead, seeing what her character would have seen, she could understand getting swept up into the holiday spirit. Christmas was completely different here than anywhere else she'd been, and it made sense to fall all the way back into that if you came from it.

Heck, she'd only been here two days and she was feeling nostalgic for a romance she'd never had. That must be what was making her all giddy-adult-woman every time Matt walked in the room.

Rosalie shrugged. This wasn't really what her job was, but Jessica found pulling her friend in for all things shoot-related always had been a good bet.

"When we get to it, try out something new." Rosalie lowered her voice as if imparting a deep, dark secret. "Improvise."

There was that word she hated.

It never got you the required result. Just more guesswork and a black hole of planning.

They worked some more, Jessica trying not to admit to herself what the real issue was... until she blurted it out to Rosalie.

"I don't improvise." She thought about the mess from last night. Yeah, improvising went just as poorly for her as in real life. "I wanted the writer to script a casual conversation with the mayor."

Before Rosalie could give her an answer—probably one about it being fine and not to worry—a knock on the trailer door interrupted them and Barbara stuck her head in.

"Can I come in?" She had a phone to her ear again but looked like she was talking to Jessica, because who would ask their phone if they could come in?

"Of course."

"We have a problem." Barbara stepped in, holding the ever-present phone against her chest as if to block out their conversation—or whoever she had on the other end. "One of the cameras is broken."

Okay. *Don't panic*. Cameras break. They were on a tight schedule, but they could do this.

"How long to get it fixed?"

"At least an hour. And we're supposed to be finished by seven tonight."

"We can shoot with one camera." Not convenient, but sadly, that was a fairly normal state of affairs. "It will just take longer."

Barbara shook her head and Jessica couldn't help but worry what was coming.

"They'll have to delay their snowman-building competition."

Jess could tell Barbara wanted her to okay it, that she didn't see the reason to reschedule the shoot for a snowman-building night. But Jess couldn't think of worse news. Not after hearing all about it on the tour.

"Oh, no." How in the world was she going to convince Matt they would stay out of the town's way like this? "We can't do that to them. Not after the tree and the Santa."

The look on Sophie's face when she thought they'd done something to Santa had just about killed her.

"If we stop now, I don't know how we'll catch up." Barbara shook her head. She'd obviously been putting a lot of thought into this. "We're already going to be pushing to get everything in before the twenty-third."

"You're going to go over budget," Rosalie chimed in from where she still sat at her makeshift desk.

"Don't worry about the budget. I'll take care of it." Because that's what producers did. They made things work. "We'll figure something out. I promised them no more surprises."

"You're the producer." Barbara gave her a shrug, obviously glad this camera issue was someone else's problem. "I'll go tell the crew we're done for the night."

"Great." Or not.

Canceling the night's shoot was not what Jessica wanted to do, but logistically, it was the only move available.

Barbara climbed out of the trailer, already back on the phone with her son, making whatever mom compromises she had to.

Rosalie gave Jessica a pat on the arm as they watched the door fall shut behind Barbara.

"Are you sure about this?" Rosalie asked.

"What other choice do I have?" Jess glanced out at the set being shut down for the night, the lights going down and the team being called off.

How could she have ever anticipated this? Sure, things went wrong on a film, but typically, the local population was so excited to have their town involved, they bent over backward to help.

Well, most of Homestead seemed excited about it from what she saw today. Unfortunately, it was their fearless leader she was going to have to talk to about it. And she didn't find herself willing to push that envelope with him after seeing the town he was trying to protect through his eyes.

Of all the places she could improvise… this was totally not the next unscripted conversation she wanted to have with him.

"I don't know, but Jess, I think you need to consider this some more." Rosalie closed her planner and folded her hands on the table. "This producing gig… it's making the hard calls. And yes—" She waved a hand between them when she saw Jessica about to interrupt. "Yes, you made the tough decision today, but I'm going to ask you: was it the right one, or was it the one where you don't upset anyone?"

"Barbara was plenty annoyed."

"She was, but not really. It's not her call, so it doesn't matter. You're her boss *and* if this backfires, you take the heat, not her." Rosalie gave her a little smile, obviously worried about her. "But if you'd made the other decision, the one that would have postponed the snowman competition, you would have had people irritated with you... or maybe just one person."

Jessica sat back, surprised Rosalie thought she was taking the easy way out.

This was anything but easy. It was downright difficult. And true, Matt would've been more upset than the crew... *tonight.* But if she didn't keep them on schedule, the holidays could be ruined for everyone. Eventually, the crew was going to be unhappy with the outcome of postponing shoots and moving the schedule around. If they didn't get everyone home by Christmas Eve, she was sure that they would be more than a little irritated. They'd be flat-out mad.

"I hear what you're saying, Rosalie, but I'm thinking big-picture here. If we get too far off schedule, we're going to need to be in the town's good graces."

Rosalie looked at her for a long moment before giving a sharp nod. "Okay. Well then, I'm glad you made the call. I'll see you back at the lodge."

She let the door fall shut behind her, leaving Jessica to finish her notes for the night.

After Jess ran them over to Barbara, she'd ask Gavin to go get the car and end this very long day before someone else had an emergency.

CHAPTER NINE

T he snowman competition was always one of the best nights of the year. When Matt had been a kid, he and his dad and Zoe would make the worst snowman in town while his mom cheered them on with hot chocolate at the ready. It was one of his favorite memories.

If only their parents were here this year.

"I think our snowman should have blue eyes." Sophie grabbed his hand and gave it a tug. "So he'll be special."

He smiled down at his daughter, the only person he knew who would think of a blue-eyed snowman. This was why he loved Christmas. And new traditions added to the old kept the joy in the family.

"Our snowman is always special." Matt didn't feel the need to add that it was because they'd made it together. Years of dad-ing had taught him not to say that if he didn't want to get an eye roll in return.

"Dad." Sophie gave him one of the deep sighs that made him wonder just how much worse the teen years would be. "It always looks like a blob."

Matt slid a look toward Zoe, knowing exactly where that early attitude had come from. Sometimes it felt like his daughter was Zoe's mini-me.

As if reading his mind, she shrugged and gave him a cocky smile. "I don't know where she gets it."

He watched as Zoe's smile dropped away and she glanced toward the paparazzi taking photos at the edge of the crowd. When the photographer waved at her, she gave him a glare and turned away.

"What was that all about?" Matt crossed his arms, staring the guy down from beside his irate sister.

"Nothing." She brought her typical smile back out. "Just wish the vultures would leave the normal folk alone."

Before Matt could figure out what that meant, Pete was shouting to quiet the crowd.

"Everyone!" Pete was at the front of the crowd, waving his hands for quiet. "Could I have your attention? We'll be starting promptly at seven o'clock. This is your fifteen-minute warning!"

Matt glanced around, gauging the competition. It was true; they'd never won before. Okay. They'd never even placed before. He was pretty sure the town was about to give them a third-generation pity-prize. But still, it was always a great night.

Maybe Sophie was old enough to redeem them this year—*blue eyes. Huh.*

"Oh hey." Rosalie wove through the crowd when she spotted him. "Mr. Mayor."

Again with the Mr. Mayor. Everyone was starting to do it.

"Please, it's Matt."

"Listen, I just wanted to let you know that we're going to be done any minute now." She gave him a little smile he read as half apology, half humor-the-crazy-guy-who-didn't-want-the-movie-people-here. "Jessica insisted on it."

"She did?" That surprised him. He thought everything and everyone came after her movie.

"Yes. She's going to make sure there aren't any more problems." Rosalie was very good at this reassuring-smile thing.

"Well... that's great." Huh, they really were willing to work with them. "Thank you."

"Have a great night." She gave him another one of her nods and headed off.

"See?" Zoe bumped his shoulder. "She's not so bad after all."

Matt couldn't help but agree. He would have expected Jessica to charge forward, getting her movie done as quickly as possible. He'd assumed she'd be all business rushing in and taking over—of course, the mistaken identity moment at the bakery had solidified that thought.

Maybe he was wrong—about a lot of things.

He glanced over in time to see Jessica, looking

exhausted and a bit defeated, making her way to her trailer. If he ever was going to apologize, now was the time.

The countdown to the snowman-building competition was on. This was their year. Matt could feel it.

He glanced toward Sophie and Zoe doing... nothing snowman-related. Okay. Maybe this wasn't their year.

The girls were right. The Larson family made a blob every year. They'd probably never win. Luckily, that wasn't what mattered.

He glanced around the crowd, feeling so happy to be there... so happy to be their mayor.

She'd pulled the strings to make sure they stayed on schedule. She'd made sure the town had been able to keep this.

He realized suddenly that not only did he have to apologize, but he had to do it right then.

"Zoe, keep an eye on Sophie." He handed the snowman making kit to Sophie.

"Where are you going?" Sophie tugged his sleeve. "The contest is going to start."

"Don't worry. I'll be right back." He glanced up, trying to spot Jessica in the crowd.

When he didn't, he wandered through the gathering a moment before deciding to try her trailer. This wouldn't take long. In and out. Apologize and get back to the important stuff. No problem.

He owed her, and he wasn't a man to put off his debts.

Thank goodness the day was over. Jessica didn't think she could take one more unscheduled event. She loved her job, but the strain of producing too had definitely weighed on her today. But she'd made the decision, and she thought it was the right one.

The cast and crew were always reminded when they went on location that they were guests, but this was the first time it had ever really been driven home. Usually, they were so welcomed that they had to keep people from wanting to help instead of having to win them over.

Of course, she'd never shot in a small town before, and she was definitely getting a clearer view of behind the scenes this time around.

She was beginning to realize that Matt felt like he needed to look out for the people there. He wasn't just being a stick-in-the-mud. He was actually protecting those who weren't really protecting themselves.

Maybe, if she weren't in movies, she might have hated the disruption, also.

She glanced around at the set, the hustle and bustle, the creative energy coming off everyone there, and knew that—no. She'd love it even if she were just watching from the outside.

But she couldn't help but respect Matt's desire

to protect his community. She'd become too used to people doing what was best for them or their careers that it had been hard at first to respect someone who was doing what he thought was right for others.

When she saw Gavin on the edge of the square, she headed his way and asked him to bring the car around. It was odd to be using the car in such a small place, but Rosalie had suggested it, knowing that, by the end of the day, Jess might not be able to keep that friendly smile on her face. Not to mention that since Ian was here already, they found themselves expecting more paparazzi at any moment.

She waited at the edge of the set, her attention snagged by the crowd gathered on the square.

All the families and friends were having a ball. This town didn't seem to have a lot of social divides, and she found herself gravitating toward their fun, her gaze naturally searching out Matt's tall person rising just above the rest of the crowd.

Her phone flashed Jill's name. It was like she knew she needed a friend today. Perfect timing.

"Jill! Hi."

"Hey…"

Oh, that didn't sound good.

"What's wrong?" She really wasn't sure she could manage someone else's problems today, too.

Jessica shook it off. That wasn't how friends loved on friends. Her bad day could wait.

"Nothing," Jill answered, sounding not as sure about that as she insisted. "Everything is great." Before

Jessica could say anything, Jill hurried on. "Here's the thing... Michael and I got back together, soooo..."

She let it sit out there unfinished.

"So, you're not coming with me to Fiji," Jessica filled in for her, because Jill's silence forced her to.

"Well, I'm actually going to Florida with Michael to see his family."

Jessica couldn't believe it. Less than two weeks till Christmas, and she was getting dumped by her best friend.

"Please be happy for me."

"I am." Jessica just couldn't help but wonder who would be happy for her, though. She was looking at a Christmas alone now.

She shouldn't be upset. She shouldn't even be surprised. But she couldn't help it. She had really been looking forward to a best girlfriends' holiday. It would have been a great treat after her last few holidays, when she'd been dating Vince. She'd not only been looking forward to this, she was beginning to think she needed it. Going home didn't feel like an option because it created chaos for her family.

Not only did the paparazzi follow her home, but she did not have one of those they-still-treat-me-the-same type of hometowns. You'd think she hadn't had her first scraped knee there, first horrible crush, those absolutely terrible bangs she'd cut herself... everything that made her just one of the girls, before she'd been "discovered" one day at the mall.

It wasn't as if she'd done it on purpose to spite her

friends, but they had such different lives that it had been easier to grow apart than stick together.

And so she'd thought a girls' week, just her and Jill, would have been the perfect downtime without the stress that came with annoying everyone with her presence and what it brought.

She glanced back at the town square and all the love between the groups there and felt her heart crack a bit.

"Please be happy for me. I need my best friend to be happy for me…"

Jessica tried to keep her voice positive. What was done was done. "Yeah, I am."

She paused and Jill said nothing, making her fill in the silence again, putting all of it on Jess. She swept the unfairness of that away and perked up her voice.

"Jill, they're calling me back to the set. Okay. Love you. Bye."

Before Jill could find her voice this time, Jessica hung up, trying to remind herself that this didn't mean she was alone. She was just between plans—that one more person was expecting her to improvise.

Improvise Christmas? Not really what she'd intended on.

The laughter rising up from the competition getting ready to start in the square pulled her attention. She couldn't imagine this town or any of its people wanting an "easy, unobtrusive" holiday over a holiday where all their loved ones were there.

She was learning pretty quickly that the town *was* family.

Instead of waiting on the edge of the snowman-making crowd for Gavin, she turned and headed toward her trailer. She pushed the tears back until she was safely inside. This was not what she needed.

Why was everything going wrong this week? She just wanted to make a good movie and not be so alone during Christmas.

That felt like a fairly low bar.

She let the door shut behind her and collapsed onto the trailer's dining room bench, letting her head drop onto the table.

Five minutes.

That was all the time she'd give herself to wallow, and then she'd head back out there, find Gavin, and go on with the plan to win over the mayor and finish this movie on time and as close to budget as possible.

There was a knock on the door.

"What?" She couldn't believe someone was bothering her now. Hadn't everyone left for the night?

"Hey, I just wanted to—" Matt stuck his head inside the trailer, then, spotting her, stopped dead. "I am so sorry. I'm just—"

He motioned behind him as if he were going to back out and disappear forever.

"No, no, no. Please... come in." Jessica swept a hand over her face. This was the last person she wanted to see her with smeared makeup and puffy eyes. "Uh, what are you doing here?"

"I just wanted to…" Matt stepped into the trailer, glancing around and looking more uncomfortable than before—which, seeing as they'd started off on the worst possible footing, was saying something. "Are you okay?"

"Yeah, of course. Yup, totally fine."

He obviously wasn't buying it.

"I'm sorry to bother you." He took a step back toward the door again.

"No, seriously. It's okay. Come on in." She waited until he came the rest of the way up the stairs, and then asked, "Have a seat. What can I do for you?"

"I just wanted to say thank you." Matt came in and sat on the couch, where she joined him. "Also, wow. This is really nice."

"So, what's up?" She didn't want to shove him out the door, but she could feel the tears pushing up again.

"Your publicist told me that you were watching out for us tonight. The snowman competition?"

At least she'd done something right today.

"It's nothing." She shrugged, trying to play it off.

She didn't need him to know what the time might cost them—or her. It was horrible to think this way, but she was glad Rosalie had told him. She couldn't help but want him to think well of her.

"I know our Christmas traditions must seem silly to you…"

"No, I don't think they're silly." Jessica shook her head, suddenly appreciating them and being able to depend on them more than she had earlier that day.

"Christmas traditions are wonderful. I wish I had some."

But no. She couldn't even get her best friend to keep vacation plans with her.

She burst into tears again, devastated that Matt was there to witness it.

Matt tried to figure out what to do. "Oh. No. No, no. It's okay." He slid over to join her on her couch. "It's uh…" Finally, he caved and put an arm around her, not unlike he'd do for Sophie or Zoe.

Jessica gave an uncomfortable laugh through her tears. "I'm sorry." She wiped her eyes again and laughed. "I don't usually cry in front of strangers." She hurried to her dressing table mirror to check out the damage.

"Don't worry about it." He searched for something to put her at ease, since obviously, *Don't worry about it* wasn't going to be enough. "I've done worse in front of strangers."

Jessica gave him a look that clearly said she didn't believe him and asked, "Like what?"

"Um…" Matt searched his memory for the stupidest thing he'd done in front of other people. A surprisingly long list came to mind. He had no idea what made him grab at the most personal one. "I sang karaoke."

"Karaoke?"

"Yeah, I was…" How in the world did he start telling her this story? Maybe it was because something about her felt familiar, like he could share anything with her. "It was not long after my wife passed away, and I was in Chicago for a travel industry thing. There was this little karaoke bar, and for some reason, it became very important to me to sing a Celine Dion song."

Jess let out a surprised laugh. He grinned, pleased with the reaction, his heart rolling over a bit.

He remembered that night all too well. His wife had loved that song. She didn't care how cheesy he thought her love songs were. She said they were real.

And he loved Melanie, so that was all that mattered.

"Come on. Really?" she asked with a laugh.

"Yeah, sadly, this is all true. Luckily, no videos have turned up on the internet yet, so I think I may have gotten away clean." He gave her the grin that used to get him out of trouble with his mother. "Now you're the only one who knows that."

"Well, your secret is safe with me."

"Thank you. So is yours." He paused, taking in how real she was in that moment. "With me. You know… the crying secret."

"Thank you."

"And, thank you again for making it so we could have tonight's competition. The snowmen are grateful." And so was he.

"Good luck with the competition."

"Yeah, we're going to need it." He shrugged as if it weren't as bad as all that. "Or so I've been told."

She smiled again, probably wanting him to just leave already. But, when he got to the door, her hand fell on his arm and stopped him.

"Matt, I just wanted to say thank you for talking to me. You made me feel a lot better." She leaned in and kissed him on the cheek.

He tried not to read anything into it, but he could still feel the light brush of her lips on his cheek, smell the soft rose scent she wore, feel the closeness of her.

Matt glanced around the trailer again, grasping for something to ground him and realizing her RV was nicer than anything he'd ever seen—also, not very Homestead. Instead, it was completely modern with everything someone might want while living or working out of it for weeks at a time.

But she'd done enough work today. And he hated to leave her here alone and sad.

Who was he kidding? He hated to leave her, period.

"So..." Matt tried not to grin as Jessica suddenly looked nervous. "Would you like to come with us to the snowman-building competition? I mean, it's just me and Sophie and my sister building a snowman... nothing flashy."

Instead of brushing him off, she gave him a broad smile. "Give me a minute to change out of wardrobe?"

"Sure." He sat back, taking in the trailer as a whole as he waited for her.

Not only did he think she needed a little more

Christmas in her life, but maybe if she saw how amazing the holidays were in Homestead, she'd appreciate why it was important.

Plus, he couldn't wait to see the California girl trying to make a giant snowball.

Win-win.

Chapter Ten

Outside the trailer's window, Ian snapped the shot of Jessica leaning in and kissing Matt. Wow. This was crazy. No one was going to believe this. Weird angle, but she was obviously kissing the guy.

He clicked away, getting as many shots of the moments after as he dared. He was so made. Not only was he the only one here, but he got a picture no one else would have any clue about. He'd probably be able to retire on this.

Like that Princess Kate sunbathing picture another guy shot a few years ago.

Of course, that had brought an ugly lawsuit and the photog being blacklisted, so just a kiss was probably for the best.

He jumped off the trash can he'd pulled over to her window and whipped his phone out, hitting Mickey's speed dial.

"Ian, this better be good."

"Well, hello to you, too." Ian glanced through the photos, picking the three he'd forward on to Mickey for now. If he wanted to see more, that was an easy fix. "I'm sending you something right now. Check it out."

He checked the WiFi on his camera and sent over his top choices. He waited while he listened to Mickey click around as the photos went through.

"Holy cow! Who is this guy?"

"You're not going to believe this." Ian glanced over his shoulder, rushing away and hoping to avoid Gavin as he went. The last thing he needed was to get his camera broken, even if he'd already sent the money shots on. "He's the local innkeeper. Life imitating art much?"

Mickey snorted. That was probably even the angle he'd use to sell it.

"I'm packing up and heading back in the morning." Ian couldn't think beyond that. He'd have to change a lot of things—probably move and figure out what to do next—but even after splitting the proceeds with Mickey, the cash payout for getting the first picture of America's most famous actress kissing someone after her recent breakup would be worth big bucks.

"You absolutely are not coming back tomorrow." He could hear Mickey furiously typing in the background. "You're the only guy up there. If anything else happens before the other guys start showing up, that's two exclusives. We can sell the first one and auction the second one."

Not what Ian wanted to hear, but it made sense.

"Get me the high-res stuff." Mickey was already half off the phone. "I can't show these to anyone until they see the quality, too. I don't want us ending up with a lame *Enquirer* cover when we could get *People* or *Us Weekly*."

"No problem. As soon as I'm done for the night, I'll send it on."

Ian wasn't surprised when he didn't get a good-bye, just the dead end of a cell phone when Mickey hung up. But who cared as long as he could get his cash and be free of this life and Mickey? That was all that mattered.

He headed back down the alley, knowing if Jessica saw him after that, she'd have her people all over him.

And he'd seen what happened to great photos that were fought over before they could go live. First, the celebrity's people called, offering money, and then they offered a lawsuit. Magazines would either double down or back away, depending on the story. But either way, the story would be leaked and out there before the photo. A total lost opportunity.

So, Ian tucked his camera away and headed back to his room to proof the shots. He had to stay on top of this, quietly.

Then he could get on with his own life.

CHAPTER ELEVEN

M att could finally see what his family meant by the whole snow-blob thing.

"We need more snow for the base." He pointed at the not-quite-round thing Jessica was working on.

"I thought this was the head." She looked at her work of art with even more dismay.

"No, that's the head." Zoe pointed at a ball of snow that was already too big to be the head—unless they were building the King Kong version of a snowman.

They all stood for a moment, looking at their collection of snowman parts, when Matt realized they had even less going for them than he thought. One… two… three… four… five. Why did they have five snow body parts? Shouldn't they have three?

"We're in so much trouble." Sophie shook her head, obviously resigned to the fact that Larson adults—even with Jessica's help—could not be trusted with snowman competitions.

"No, come on." Jessica turned to Sophie and handed her more snow. "We can do this! Let's work on the body. Here."

"That's the base!" Matt wasn't sure they'd pull this off. They couldn't even figure out how to put together a snowman.

"Okay, time check." Jessica glanced around, looking for a countdown or something. "How much time do we have left?"

He checked his watch. "Twenty minutes."

"We are in so much trouble." Sophie shook her head, disappointed but not surprised because… blob.

"No." Jessica shook her head, trying to be encouraging while side-eyeing the snow blob.

"We can do this, right, Soph?" Matt patted some more snow on what he thought was the base.

"You know, this would be easier if this was an actor. Then we could cover up his flaws with hair and makeup and… *wardrobe*." Jessica's head shot up as she glanced at Matt and grinned.

What was she—Oh! Yes!

"Come on!" Jessica took off, weaving through the crowd and breaking into a run toward the production trailers. The crew seemed more than a little surprised to see them rushing past, but Jessica was at the head, so they let them go by. "Excuse me! Hi. Coming through. Need to borrow a few things."

Jessica started grabbing things and throwing them at whichever Larson was closest. Matt was afraid to touch anything. The well-organized prop trailer was never going to look the same. Sophie went to pull something down, but he took her hand, unsure if they should really be "helping" right now.

"What about that?" Sophie pointed at a fancy hat with a feather coming out of the top.

"Yes!" Jessica pulled the overdone costume piece down and plopped it onto Sophie's head. "Come on, you guys! We have less than twenty minutes!"

With permission granted, they each grabbed a few things to add to the pile. As they rushed back to their blob, the other competitors stopped to stare at them and their arms filled with props and costumes. At their area, Sophie took charge, pointing to places that needed to be decorated or hidden. When the buzzer rang, they all stepped back, ignoring the extra snow blobs they'd kicked to the side.

"Nice." Zoe nudged Matt shoulder to shoulder. "I mean, it's probably still a blob, but no one can tell under this incredible wardrobe."

"I like him." Sophie reached up and straightened his blue eyes. "I really like the hat."

Matt stood flanked by his two girls and glanced over at Jessica. Her tears were gone, replaced by a happy smile. But as she looked around, he could see the distance between them for what it was—more of an ocean than a puddle.

Pete started walking down the aisles, commenting on each snowman and praising the families or teams who made them.

"Nice. Good craftsmanship." Pete moved on, getting closer to them. "Well done, team! Impressive."

When he reached theirs, he paused, turning every which way to look at all the accessories the snowman was working. The costume and wig were attention-grabbing enough, but Sophie had insisted their snowperson needed makeup to go with the blue eyes.

Pete glanced at the other judges, studying the snowman closely before they all stepped away.

"We have a winner!" He waved his hand at their well-dressed blob.

Sophie was the first to start jumping up and down, shouting that they won. After high fives all around, Jessica gave a blushing Pete a hug as Sophie claimed their trophy.

She leaned in to her dad and said, "Hailey Shephard is going to die when I bring this to school."

They'd have to have a talk about that later.

As they drove back to the lodge in Jessica's SUV, the celebration continued until they got home.

Zoe steered Sophie toward the innkeepers' quarters. "Come on, Soph. Time for bed."

"Okay." She grinned up at Jess, obviously starting to feel a bit more normal around her. "Night, Jessica. Thanks for making our snow blob better!"

"My pleasure." She pointed at the metal snowman Sophie carried. "Put that trophy somewhere special."

Matt stopped at the top of the stairs, letting Sophie and Zoe move ahead of them. "I'll be right in."

Sophie bounced ahead as Zoe gave him a look that

clearly questioned what he was doing. He watched them go, the trophy catching the gleam of the Christmas lights framing the porch.

"I think she's going to sleep with that tonight." He couldn't help but run through all the "prizes" his daughter had dragged into her bed over the years.

"Tonight?" Jess laughed at him, and he realized that, yes, Sophie would probably sleep with it longer than that. "When I won my Golden Globe, I slept with it for a week."

"You won a Golden Globe?" He added a *huh* on the end, interested and yet not surprised.

"Wow." Jess shook her head, an oddly pleased smile on her face. "You really don't know who I am, do you?"

"I know who you are." He gave her a wink, as if it were a secret. "You were in that one movie with the dragons. And then there was that other movie with the dragons."

"Oh yes." Jess gave him a nod as if he knew what he was talking about. "Who could forget that one?"

"Okay, you're right." Matt suddenly realized she wasn't the girl who had barged into the bakery. That this *friendship* or whatever it was they had didn't rely on her being famous. "I don't know who you are."

Holding out her hand, she introduced herself. "I'm Jessica McEllis."

"Matt Larson."

His hand slid into hers, probably more callused than the polished, manicured hands she was used to holding. "Nice to meet you."

"You too."

They stood in companionable silence, letting the moment draw out. It was as if neither knew if they should move forward or step back—yet, stillness seemed to be the motion they fell into, comfortable but new.

A heavy *click* of a door pulled shut more loudly than necessary broke into their bubble.

"Hey, you two." Vince stood at the top of the stairs, smiling down at them. "What's going on?"

Matt dropped her hand as she stepped back.

"We were just celebrating our win at the snowman competition tonight." She flashed her grin from one man to the other, glowing with their recent win.

"That's great." Vince turned his gaze toward him. "Matt, you should teach me how to build a snowman."

"Ah, sure." Because a grown man needed another grown man to teach him snowman building skills?

"I could put one at the top of Mount Everest when I climb it," Vince continued, "again."

Matt wasn't really sure what to say to that since he had no interest in climbing Mount Everest and he didn't know anyone else who did.

"Jess, we should probably turn in." Vince held his hand out to her, all but forcing her to end the evening. "It's an early day tomorrow."

"Yeah, okay." She turned away from Vince to glance Matt's way. "Good night, Matt. Thanks again for inviting me."

"Of course." It seemed so obvious to have invited her now.

"I had fun."

"Thanks for joining us."

She gave him a little wave and headed in, leaving him to watch them go. As the glass-framed front door to his lodge fell shut behind them, he tried not to growl as Vince's arm wrapped around Jessica's shoulders.

After they went inside, he stood, waiting for the rest of the visitors to close themselves in their rooms.

Then, as he was wont to do, he went through the lodge, closing doors, adjusting windows, checking locks, and turning lights off or putting them on their dimmer.

As he got to the parlor, he spotted Sophie's iPad and thought about Jessica, her world, and her night with them ending too soon.

Before he knew it, he was on the couch in their dimly lit parlor watching *Asterlight*, enthralled by Jessica and her power in the role.

He lost track of time as he gasped, quietly whispering a warning to her character, "Look out!" and cheered as she battled her way to the end.

CHAPTER TWELVE

I an tried to keep his voice even as Mickey went on about the picture he'd sent him, demanding the full-res picture for sale.

Ian wasn't sure why he'd held on to the photo for almost two days. He'd made a jackpot shot, and not only would it get him out of the frozen tundra he was stuck in at the moment, but the pay from a sale would give him enough after his cut to try some other things.

Apparently, Mickey had been soft-selling them all over town, hinting that they had something big about Jessica and her love life but not giving details.

He even thought Ian was holding out because once the story broke, the town would be flooded with other photographers—no matter how cold it was there. Mickey went as far as calling him a "smart kid, always thinking big-picture."

And, seriously, could it get any better? The parallels between the story she was shooting and the one unfolding here on-set were so good that even *TMZ* would be salivating for a report. He'd stick around and maybe get to do the camera report if they got their butts up here.

He was made.

And yet...

"Are you listening to me, Ian?" Mickey's typical impatience was not blunted by the fifteen-hundred-mile separation.

"Yeah. It's great, Mickey." The deal *was* great, but something ate at his stomach. Just as he was wondering what it was, he spotted Zoe walking down the opposite side of the street. "Okay, keep me posted. Bye."

Without a chance for Mickey to push anything else, he hit END and dodged the slow-moving traffic to catch up with her, because a guy's got to have his priorities.

He fell in step with her, waiting for the greeting she should have bubbled up at him. Instead, she just gave him a look and kept walking.

"My knee is much better, by the way," he said as if she'd greeted him and asked him about it.

"You owe me an ice pack, by the way," Zoe answered, still walking, giving him nothing to work with.

He liked this girl. Smooth and funny, nothing seemed to ruffle her, and she didn't let him get away with anything.

"I'll put it on my shopping list." He kept his longer stride shorter to match hers, watching her basically ignore him as the sun glinted off those curls and the cold air painted her cheeks rosy. Knowing there wasn't anything—or anyone—like this in Hollywood, he started snapping pictures.

After a moment, Zoe realized what he was doing and waved a hand between them. "Cut it out."

"Oh, come on." He took another shot as her eyes sparked annoyance at him. "I need some good stuff for my next show."

That stopped her and drew out her curiosity. "You do shows? Of celebrity photos?"

"No." He grinned at her over his lens. "I just take pictures of regular people who inspire me."

Before she could respond, he snapped another photo.

Zoe rolled her eyes at him—which, of course, he took a picture of. "I can't inspire you. You don't even know me."

Ian lowered the camera, watching her steadily as they walked on. Before he could explain, she grabbed his arm, pulling him toward her with a, "Look out!"

Apparently, light posts didn't move out of the way just because an artist was studying his new muse.

"Inspiration is unpredictable."

She slowed, looking at him, weighing his words. Ian had never wanted someone to believe him so much in his life. She made all the actresses with their made-up looks and their overly polished fronts seem frumpy in spirit. When she finally let her head drop forward so her hair covered her smile, he snapped another one.

"Stop!" She shook her head, but all he could do was stare at her through the lens.

"This is definitely going in my next show." Before she could argue with him, he lowered his camera and turned away, calling at her over his shoulder. "Bye, Zoe."

He couldn't help glancing back as he made it to the far sidewalk to see her smiling to herself.

This day couldn't get much better than a pretty girl and a good paycheck on the way.

Jessica was having a thought she'd never had before: Thank goodness for the heat from all the lights.

She was definitely method acting since she was freezing right now. The temperature had immediately dropped fifteen degrees when the sun fell behind the trees. She wished she'd accepted that extra layer from the dresser, but two hours ago, she'd only kind of needed it, not really-really-really needed it.

She and Vince were sitting on a bench in the middle of the square, filming a scene with all of the crew around them. Behind the tech guys, a good portion of the town milled around, watching the action. She never got over the weird bubble surrounding a scene— organized chaos and lots of prying eyes studying what would be an intimate moment. But sitting out there, not bundled into the crowd, the wind was cutting through her layers.

"Andddd…" Barbara's voice came from behind the camera. "Action!"

"I'm freezing!" Jessica, as her character, told Vince.

It was always odd, that moment stepping into character. Sometimes it was a small hop—like tonight. And sometimes it was quick, hard fall off a cliff.

"I'm getting you a parka for Christmas," Vince answered.

"You're getting me a present?"

"Why not?"

"We haven't seen each other since…"

"We dated in high school." He bumped her shoulder, making the characters' connection complete. He'd always been good at the little stuff like that—on-screen. "Just because you ran off to be a movie star after I broke up with you…"

He shrugged as if to say, no big deal.

"You didn't break up with me!" She channeled the outrage every girl everywhere felt when a guy pulled crap like that. "*I* broke up with *you*."

He grinned at her. "That's not the way I tell it."

She stumbled a bit—that grin used to turn her stomach to mush.

When she'd first gotten to Hollywood, Vince was already a young, rising action star. He'd been everywhere—every red carpet, every magazine cover, every after-party. She'd been working her butt off just to get invites at that point. After a few years of struggling to make it big, she'd landed the lead in a romantic comedy and then found out Vince was her co-star.

She'd cried for three days.

And not with joy.

Who was going to see a romantic comedy with macho action star Vince Hawkins as the male lead?

But they had. In droves. And a partnership had been born.

A lot of his success had been the extra time he'd taken—not just helping her as the up-and-comer, but in really nailing his role. She'd found out later he'd watched all twenty-five of the Twenty-Five Most Memorable Romantic Comedies and worked secretly with an acting coach to change some of his movement and blocking habits.

That movie had been where she'd first started respecting him as a peer. The fact that she liked him didn't hurt, either. And he was so darn pretty to look at. Vince was just a nice guy.

But, not *the* nice guy. She tried not to think of Matt, but he jumped into her head, and she almost missed her cue.

"I think you're misting the point." *Crud. Stupid word.* She laughed, trying to play off the flub. "Misting? What is misting?"

Vince glanced down at her and joined in the laughter. They'd almost always been able to laugh off the stupid stuff on-set. She hadn't realized how lucky she was until she'd done her next movie. That guy had been a different experience. Even his funny bone hadn't had a sense of humor.

That was one of the reasons she'd pushed for them to hire Vince. He was not only professional, but easy to work with. She needed a little "easy" on this first producing gig.

Barbara's voice jumped in. "Cut! Let's reset."

The crew rushed around, setting up to reshoot. Jess always felt bad about that—especially when, like tonight, she was off her game, creating more work for everyone.

"Sorry!" she shouted to the group at large.

Barbara waved it off as she marched toward a set of guys in the corner to give some drilled-down instructions.

"Do you remember what I got you?" Vince asked out of context, pulling her attention back to him. "For our last Christmas together?"

Of course, she did; he gave them to her last year. "Earrings."

She glanced at Vince out of the side of her eye, wondering where yet another walk down memory lane this week was headed.

"Antique earrings." He clarified. "With sapphire insets. Your birthstone."

"They are lovely."

Vince waited a moment before asking, "Do you still wear them?"

"Sometimes." Jessica thought about the earrings. They really were lovely. Not something you could wear regularly, but still. "You always had great taste in presents."

"Wait until you see what I got you this year." Vince suddenly sounded like a ten-year-old kid. "I know, I shouldn't be getting you a gift, but I saw it and you said you liked it once..."

"You remembered I said I liked something... and got it for me?"

Jessica was suddenly curious again what exactly was going on here.

"I know you think that I never listened to you, but I did." He shifted to puppy dog eyes. Darn it; he was good. "So, are you going to make me take it back?"

She should, but they were still friends and co-workers. She was slightly embarrassed she didn't get him something now that she knew he'd gotten her a present.

"No." She glanced at him, sitting comfortably at her side, obviously pleased with himself. "It was very thoughtful of you."

"You want to go out to dinner?"

That seemed like a weird shift. Jessica was trying to slow down her thoughts enough to try to figure out where Vince's mind was.

"Tonight? I can't. I'm going on the carriage ride with the Larsons."

She studied the action behind the camera, not meeting Vince's gaze so he couldn't read anything into her expression.

"The who?"

Jessica felt all the goodwill he'd been building drop right out of her body. How did he not know who the

Larsons were? Not only were they being incredibly hospitable to people she wasn't even sure they all wanted in their lodge, but Matt was the mayor.

The kink in the plan, the thing she had to make work to keep the town happy. The business part of this business plan.

Plus, Zoe, who was the sweetest human on the planet, and Sophie, the most adorable.

Was Vince really that trapped in his own world to not know who their hosts were?

"The people who run the lodge." She waited for him to jump in. "You know, Zoe and Sophie..."

"And Matt." Vince suddenly sounded grumpy. So he did know.

"Yes. Matt."

"Okay, then. Cool. That sounds like fun." All of Vince's warmth dripped away, leaving just clipped annoyance. "Another night then."

Jessica turned to look at her formerly pleasant co-worker and wondered again—what the heck was going on?

CHAPTER THIRTEEN

When evening finally came, Jess was surprisingly looking forward to the carriage ride. It wasn't something she could—or even more importantly—*would* have done back in L.A.

She'd watched a family take off just a moment ago, and the kids look as excited as she felt.

Glancing around, she couldn't help but love the idea that everyone was milling about in front of the lodge, enjoying hot chocolate and chatting about their plans for the rest of the week. Everyone was having fun just hanging out awaiting their turn. Before she knew it, she and Matt and Sophie were finally at the front of the line and next to get the carriage. The wait had been more pleasant than she could have imagined. Especially since they'd put heat lamps on the porch for those standing still.

"Hey, Jessica." Sophie gave a tug on her jacket from where she stood between her and Matt. "Did you know that Hailey Shephard—this girl in my class—has a horse?"

She wasn't really sure what the right answer to that was.

"I did not know that." Well, that seemed to be a valid answer. Go with the obvious.

"We're not getting a horse," Matt said.

"Of course not!" Sophie sounded obviously shocked. Either she was an even better actress than Jessica, or she was actually appalled by the idea. "That would be copying. We need something special. Like a zebra."

"A zebra would be special."

"We're not getting a zebra, either." Matt gave her a you're-not-helping look and said, "Where would we get a zebra anyway?"

She shot him a grin over Sophie's head. Of course, she could think of several people who would get her a zebra, but this might not be the time to mention that.

She was biting her tongue when the carriage pulled up and the last set of riders climbed down.

Jess was pleasantly surprised when Matt handed her up into the carriage himself instead of letting the driver do it. She tried to tell herself she was imagining things, but she was almost sure he held her hand longer than he needed to. After that, he lifted Sophie in behind her, who immediately leaned on the back of the driver's box to get a "good view."

Jess's breath caught as Matt settled in next to her. This guy who had no idea who she was, who didn't care about her fame or money or what she did for a living, made her heart race a bit faster than was probably good or safe, knowing she was leaving in a few days.

"Here we go!" The driver tipped his hat to them before facing forward and urging the horses onward.

With a slight jerk, the carriage rolled onward and pulled away from the lodge. The town was beautifully lit up, and it seemed like a special silence fell over the rest of the route.

"It's beautiful." She couldn't help her gaze from darting around the town. It wasn't as if she hadn't seen it before, but the carriage ride added to the magic.

"We normally go down King Street." Matt pointed to a road off to their left.

"But the movie stuff is in the way?" she asked, already knowing the answer.

"Yeah."

Jessica felt an odd respect for Matt for not taking on the apologetic, don't-worry attitude so many people got with famous people—like just because someone with a certain job wanted to do something made it okay.

Part of her wished he would because being humored would be easier, but she was glad he didn't.

"I'm sorry. I can call…"

"It's okay. We can change things up every now and then, right?"

She looked over at him, trying to read his backpedaling apology-type-statement.

He obviously didn't like change, and this one was

just added on to the ever-growing pile. But, *thank goodness* was all Jessica could think because Barbara would kill her, and it would put them further off schedule if he had insisted they move things for the carriage rides.

And Rosalie would point out again that she was making the easy decision by pleasing the only person complaining.

Before she could figure out what to say, Sophie decided to climb up onto the bench seat with them, sitting in the middle.

"What's Christmas like in Hollywood?"

"Well... warmer than this." Jess hadn't realized how cold she was until she said it, but Iowa was all kinds of cold she hadn't really been ready for.

"Oh, sorry. Here." Matt grabbed a throw blanket off the bench facing them and tucked them all under it.

Still being sweet even when he was a little annoyed.

"Do you spend it with movie stars?" Sophie asked, pulling her attention back.

"Christmas?" Jessica shrugged. "Sometimes. There's usually a party going on somewhere."

Of course, those parties weren't really Christmas like what Sophie meant, and suddenly, that seemed to matter.

"But not this year?" Matt asked, obviously confused by this idea. She glanced around the carriage, realizing that Matt was tied not just to tradition, but to specific ones for the town and his family.

"No. I mean, I could spend some time with my

family, but I—" Jessica thought about how crazy it got when she went home... and the fact that her parents didn't try too hard to convince her not to skip the visit. "I always seem to mess up holidays for them. They should be able to enjoy them and not have it burdened by paparazzi or fans, or—"

"You can spend it with us." Sophie grabbed her hand and gave it a tiny, child-sized squeeze, obviously meaning the invitation for more than just her own enjoyment.

Jess was amazed again how aware and generous children could be.

"Sophie..." Matt gave her a nudge in warning.

"It's a lot of fun," she rushed on. "We have the festival of lights on Christmas Eve and then I go to bed early so I can get up and we can open presents by the tree."

Jessica gave her a soft smile, trying to avoid committing since an invitation from a ten-year-old wasn't really valid. And even if Matt had added his approval, it felt like she was bringing her drama somewhere else it probably wasn't wanted. Matt couldn't wait to get the whole crew out of Homestead. She couldn't imagine him wanting one of them—especially the one who garnered the most attention—sticking around.

But, to Sophie, having your favorite actress spend one holiday with her was different than Jessica's parents having to deal with a visit and everything it brought.

"Wow, that does sound like fun," Jess said as non-committedly as possible.

"Sophie," Matt stepped in before the little holiday planner could rush on, "I'm sure that Jessica has better things to do than spend Christmas in Homestead."

Sophie rolled her eyes, leaving Jessica muffling a laugh. This father-daughter dynamic was certainly something surprising. They seemed really relaxed with one another—none of that push-pull she'd expect of a single dad and his tiny partner in crime.

"What could be better than Christmas in Homestead? Look at it." Sophie waved a hand as they went by the town square, and Jessica couldn't help but admit it was stunning. "It's like... perfect."

Pictures did it no justice. The world saw these small towns through the long-distance lens of movies and storytellers. Jessica was finding out that they were so much more, in so many ways.

"Yes, it is." Her gaze met Matt's over Sophie's head, and she felt—for maybe the first time in her life—completely in accord with someone else.

"What was Christmas like when you were growing up here?" she asked Matt, changing the subject but honestly wanting to know. She couldn't imagine what it would be like to have this going on every year. Not just the planning and work, but also the anticipation and fun.

"Loud." Matt laughed. "Definitely loud. And there was always people everywhere. Singing and laughing and opening presents and eating. It was always just crazy."

That sounded... wonderful. Jessica's parents, even when she was there, were fairly subdued. Polite, polished, lovely—just like the beautiful, white-balled tree Rosalie had put up at her house.

She fought the sigh that slipped out. "That's the kind of Christmas I'd like to have."

"So why don't you?" Sophie asked.

Jessica froze, surprised by the question. How was it that kids seemed to boil things down to the most basic issue? And now she was asking herself. Yes, why didn't she?

She'd always had a reason for not having that—her parents, the paparazzi, her relationship with Vince... on and on.

Maybe the real reason was that having a Christmas like that seemed to be a family event—something solid and continuous that said *these are my people for better or worse.*

"Looks like we're almost back," Matt's voice broke into her thoughts.

She wasn't ready for it to end, any of it. Not just the ride. She realized that the shoot would soon come to a close, too. "It's done already?"

"Afraid so." Matt gave her an apologetic smile this time.

"That's too bad."

"Well..." He glanced at the line but went on anyway. "We could go again if you're not too cold."

She didn't even have to think about it. Even if she was freezing, she wasn't ready for it to end.

"Let's go around again!" Sophie voted immediately.

"I'm not too cold." Jess pushed her heart back into place. "I think I'm getting used to it. You're sure they'll let us?"

"Well, I am the mayor." Matt pretended to puff out his chest as if he'd really pull rank on anyone. He couldn't even get his town to limit the movie's access because he didn't want to railroad them. "I think I can pull some strings."

"Yeah!" Sophie settled back into her seat, making the decision a done deal.

"Okay." Jessica gave Sophie her own smile and grabbed her hand. "Yes, let's do it."

Matt gave both of them a smile and leaned down to ask the driver to go around one more time.

"Hey."

Seemingly from out of nowhere, Vince hoisted himself onto the carriage step. "Room for one more?"

"Vince?" Jessica looked at him, for the first time in who knew how long, not really able to read him. What now?

"Hi Vince!" Sophie shouted, welcoming him right aboard. "Yes, sit here!"

She pointed to the seat she'd been kneeling on earlier behind the driver—obviously offering him the extra room.

Jessica was pleased that Matt had raised such a

sweet, kind little girl willing to share, but, again, what the heck was up with Vince?

"Well." He settled in, making sure to take up at least his share of the bench. "This is cozy! Driver. Once more around the square."

The driver gave them a solid nod, and Vince and Sophie chatted away happily.

Jessica tried not to glare at him, but until she figured out what was up with him, she was suspicious of all this togetherness suddenly happening.

She was going to get to the bottom of it ASAP.

CHAPTER FOURTEEN

Z oe loved this time of night. Things were calming down, and she'd done everything to make her guests happy throughout the day. Now she could focus on the details that made Homestead Lodge special, not only to their guests, but to them.

She checked the front room, ensuring the pillows had been fluffed and the blankets straightened, adding water to the flower vase, closing the curtains for the evening—and noticed Ian standing outside, looking cold and miserable.

This guy… she did not know what to think.

But she couldn't stand to see someone—even someone with a miserable job—freezing out there alone. She grabbed a cup of hot cocoa and headed out, not questioning what she was doing. Without a word, she handed him the cup.

"What's this?" Ian looked at it, more surprised than accusatory.

"Hot chocolate." Zoe refrained from adding, *obviously*.

Ian gazed at her a long moment, stretching it out till she was about go before saying, "Thank you."

"You're welcome." She started to turn away and leave him to his own privacy-invading devices.

He stared at the steam coming off the creamy drink before glancing back up. "No marshmallows?"

Zoe stopped, making a decision. Pity only went so far, but this guy really pushed the boundaries. There was just something about him that made her want to try to fix it all. Of course, it didn't help that she was a fixer. Sure, she dreamed of a chain of lodges, but what she really wanted was to give people a restful place to rejuvenate and feel at home. But she had to draw the line somewhere with people.

"Come on." She rolled her eyes and nodded her head toward the lodge, giving him the okay to follow.

Ian followed her right up the path and into the kitchen, glancing around at the home side of the lodge. While Zoe made herself a cup and added marshmallows to it before tossing him the bag, he set his mug down and watched her bustle around.

"Thanks." He settled in, setting his camera on the table between them and taking up his cocoa.

Zoe studied him, thinking about what kind of person wouldn't mind invading other people's worlds as a job.

"What?" he asked.

"I'm just trying to figure out why someone would do what you do."

"Oh, see, and here I thought you were being nice to me." Ian sounded more than a little amused.

"I am being nice to you." Because if she wasn't, he'd still be outside freezing his tuchus off. "That's what we do here in Homestead. We're nice."

"So you insinuate that I have made questionable life choices, but you do it nicely?"

She wasn't sure how serious he was about that since even he admitted his job was horrible sometimes.

Instead, she just nodded and said, "Something like that."

"Why does what I do matter so much?"

She shrugged. She didn't know why it mattered, but she hated seeing someone being sucked into such a miserable job. It obviously wasn't making him happy.

"Nice camera," she finally landed on, to change the subject—and because it was true.

"You know cameras?" He sounded impressed. Kindness didn't do it, but liking his camera did.

Zoe knew that should tell her something.

"Melanie, my brother's late wife... was into photography."

She could hear the sadness in her own voice, and she wondered if it would ever go away. Glancing up, she saw Ian studying her. Then, with a smooth move, he slid his baby over to her.

"Take a picture," he insisted.

"What?" She looked at the camera, afraid to touch it, let alone pick it up and try to use it. "Why?"

"I thought I'd try out that 'nice' thing you were talking about."

Well, if he insisted. Maybe she could take something that really was pretty with this. She hefted the camera and was checking out the viewfinder when Ian's phone rang.

Ian glanced her way, smiling, until he looked at the phone. Then a sudden wall went up between them.

"Hey, Mickey. What? No. I'm not ready to sell that right now." He obviously didn't want to talk to whoever had called him because he rushed on, "I gotta go."

Zoe watched him disconnect the call and shove his phone in his pocket. She waited. Most people spilled some type of information about phone calls when they weren't asked, but Ian seemed to be on guard now.

Instead, she snapped a picture of the marshmallow bobbing in the hot chocolate and let him finish his in peace.

Ian's mind was obviously far, far away, so, when he was done, he walked his mug over to the sink, gave her a quick "thank you" and headed out the door looking... guilty?

Well, if a paparazzo was wandering the lodge looking guilty, she was definitely going to have to keep an eye on that.

And him.

Jessica made another loop around the ice rink, feeling awkward in front of all those people. She was used to excelling at everything she tried, but skating seemed to be her new Kryptonite.

Luckily, this was another scene shoot, and her character wasn't very good at it, either.

She tried not to glance over to where Matt, Sophie, and Zoe stood watching. She reminded herself to focus, falling back into the role as she laughed up at Vince.

They continued doing distance shots, laughing and skating and flirting. Finally, Barbara walked out onto the ice.

"Okay, cut!" She glanced around, and then continued. "We're going to do it again, so let's reset please."

Jess was more than ready to take a little break. But when she glanced over at Matt, he wasn't looking too happy about it.

She saw him lean into Pete as she neared and heard him say, "Again? They're already like an hour late."

As she pulled up to the rink's wall to join the two men, she made sure that what she was about to say was the truth.

"Relax." Zoe's voice carried across the ice as she gave her brother's arm a pat. "Everyone is having fun."

Jessica hoped that was what mattered. But she had a feeling that Matt wouldn't be able to see past his own attachment to all things the same and traditional.

Bridging the rest of the distance between her and

the rink wall, she smiled as they headed her direction, Sophie rushing to lead the way.

"This is so cool!" Sophie bounced on her toes. Being around her was so joyful. She found happiness in everything—even her competition with whichever Hailey it was who had the horse.

Sophie's excitement was contagious, but one look at Matt, and Jess felt that joy bubbling in her deflate a bit.

"We're going to be done soon and then everyone can join in," she promised.

"Great." Pete gave her a smitten grin. "I'll go let everyone know."

Sophie took her cue, and, wanting to be ready to go as soon as the opportunity arose, she all but shouted, "Zoe, let's go put on our skates!"

Jess watched them go, Zoe letting Sophie win, barely.

"I'm sorry we're running late." She mentally forced herself not to add, *again.*

The last thing she needed was to be the one reminding him that things weren't going to plan. The truth was, on a movie set, they seldom did. She just hadn't expected anyone but the producer to mind. To the cast and crew, this was business as usual. No one expected shoots to run on time. That was why they had a bit of a slush budget. Not an action-film, blockbuster slush budget, but still.

And since she was the producer…

"It's okay." Matt shrugged, looking around and

taking in the general enjoyment level. "It seems like everyone is having fun anyway."

She could all but hear him adding the previously not said *that's all that matters*. Even though she knew it wasn't true for him, no matter how much he kept telling himself that.

It was Matt who was struggling, and she felt bad about that, but at the same time, everyone *was* having a good time. It made her wonder what he felt he was protecting.

She bit her tongue to avoid pointing out that this wasn't changing their traditions. This was a year of something different, and next year, they wouldn't be back. It was a break, not *breaking*.

If only she could suck Matt into that new version of a holiday spirit.

"Are you going to skate?" she asked.

"Me?" Matt shifted his full attention back to her and grimaced. "No. Know your limitations, I always say. Maybe I'll ask Santa for coordination this year."

Jessica snorted, and not just because she knew he wanted her to laugh. She found herself laughing a lot with Matt like she didn't with anyone else. She was beginning to let her guard down around him as she only did with her inner circle.

"What did you ask Santa for?" he asked.

"A good movie," she said, and then, with a nod to one of her favorite romantic comedies, she added, "and peace on earth."

"Of course."

She rolled her eyes at him but then admitted, "I hadn't really thought about it, to be honest. I'm lucky. I have everything I need."

She knew that, in her head. She had an incredible job she loved, a team she trusted, and no worry about financial security even if this was the last role she ever played. Her family loved her, although they weren't the easygoing, close-knit clan the Larsons were. She was, in a word, blessed.

"Christmas isn't about what you need, it's about what you wish for." He glanced around, as though trying to put into words the things he'd been telling her and showing her since she arrived. "It's about…"

"Family."

"Yeah." He grinned, obviously approving of her answer. "Family."

She felt the magic bubble around them close in, shutting out the rest of the world. She and Matt were the only two in it—and the idea that he knew what Christmas was, that he could show her something new about it—was such a surprise. She'd thought he'd grasped to just the traditions and actions. She hadn't realized that here, in his town and in his heart, were deeper meanings to all of those things.

Most people, even those who loved Christmas, loved the commercial part of the holidays. The parties and gifts were where the holidays began and ended for them.

But not for Matt.

"Hey everyone!" Vince shouted as he skated past,

zooming around the rink and swishing into a fancy spin.

She wasn't surprised to see him hamming it up for the crowd, and even less so to see them eating it up. Vince was a born performer and accomplished at pretty much any physical activity out there. She should be pleased because a happy audience meant a patient audience.

During his last movie, they had to have his agent break the news to him that he couldn't do his own stunts because... possible death, blah blah blah... no training, et cetera, et cetera... and *what are you nuts?*

Glancing at Matt, she saw him watching, obviously not thrilled by Vince's show.

Men. Egos. They all had them.

"Jessica," Barbara called, breaking in before Matt could get grumpier and Vince could get showboat-ier. "We're ready."

"Yup!" she shouted back, not wanting to hold them up even more.

Matt gave her a grin as she pushed off to make her way to the center of the rink again.

"Tell Sophie to save a skate for me." She gave Matt a wave, disappointed her free time was over.

"Jessica." Rosalie waved her over, looking a little frantic as she did.

"What's wrong?"

"Nothing. I just..." Rosalie glanced around, lowering her voice. "You know we're leaving in a week. I don't want you to get too attached."

She nodded in the general direction of where the townsfolk were watching the shoot. But, Jessica was guessing she had one townsperson in mind specifically.

And maybe Rosalie was right, but there was no harm in making new friends where they were.

But she agreed. "I won't."

"Okay," Rosalie answered, still looking concerned. "I just don't want you to get hurt."

Jess didn't want that, either, but with the holiday season she was having, she wasn't sure how to avoid it. Getting over her breakup with Vince, even though it had been months, Jill canceling on her, her parents not really caring where she spent Christmas... Getting attached to the Larsons—to *Matt*—felt like just one more piece of her holiday pie this year.

"Jessica!" Barbara shouted to them. "We have to get moving."

"Okay!" She gave Rosalie a reassuring squeeze on the arm before heading back to the center of the rink.

She could only handle one thing at a time: life or work.

And right now, her whole focus was work.

Matt was pretty sure the ice skating was a hit tonight. He almost hated to admit it, but getting to skate after watching a movie being filmed right there seemed to thrill most of the townfolks. He even saw some of the little boys mimicking Vince's earlier moves.

Maybe he was missing out by not joining in.

Um, nope. He was absolutely not. He liked his feet on the ground and his butt... not.

"Excuse me?" Jessica's—what the heck was it Rosalie did?—stood in the doorway, looking more than a little worried.

He could only imagine what she was here to tell him. The thought that maybe Christmas was canceled in Homestead instead of Whoville this year rushed through his head. But then he realized that if something extreme had happened, Jessica would have told him herself.

Or, at least, he thought she would.

"Hey, Rosalie." He smiled at her, putting himself into work mode. "What can I help you with?"

He braced himself when his question made her look more uncomfortable.

"I actually wanted to talk to you... about Jessica." She sucked in a breath, obviously not excited to be there. "This is none of my business but..."

"Jessica is your business."

Which is something he'd noticed lately.

Everyone either wanted a piece of Jess or had a stake of her.

It was like her relationships all came with extra responsibilities he couldn't imagine. He loved all of his—running the lodge, raising his daughter, partnering with his slightly crazy sister, mayoring the town. They were as much the joys of his day-to-day life as they were responsibilities.

But none of that came to anything next to the weights he saw put on Jessica by people she was friendly with every day. Things that each person might think as a little thing—but little things added up to heavy weights.

He gave a quick thanks for his sister, their relationship, and their ability to balance it all with the running of Homestead Lodge.

"Yes, but I'm not here about that." Rosalie sucked in another breath, fighting through her discomfort to say whatever she'd come to say. "She's under a lot of pressure with this movie. It's important, and not just because of her career. I'm worried about, you know, unnecessary complications."

It took him a moment to realize what she was implying.

"You think I'm a complication?"

She looked surprised he'd question her. Matt couldn't help but wonder if Rosalie, as Jessica's proxy, had gotten used to people saying okay to whatever and moving on.

"She spent a lot of years building up her walls to protect herself from getting hurt."

He stared at her a long moment, realizing that this wasn't just about work for Rosalie. She genuinely thought that discussing this with him was protecting Jessica.

"But what if what's on the other side of the wall is something good?"

"I'd be all for it. I'd be leading the parade. But

Matt, we're leaving soon. And leaving is never easy for anyone. Not for her, not for you..." Rosalie smiled sadly as if she was sorry to have to be the one to say it. "Not for your daughter."

Her words found the nerve they were aimed at and pounded it to jelly. He could take risks with himself, but not with Sophie. He wasn't sure how she'd take losing another woman she cared about—even if it wasn't in a tragic way.

Maybe it was even worse to have someone choose to leave than to barely remember someone who was stolen from you.

She gave him a nod as she realized her words had been taken seriously, leaving him standing there staring after her.

He watched her go, wondering if she was worrying about nothing. It wasn't as if he expected Jessica to throw away her life in California just to get to know him and his family.

The more he thought about it, the more absurd he felt.

He set it aside, not letting himself worry about it. But Rosalie was right: some walls should stay where they were, safely protecting people on both sides.

CHAPTER FIFTEEN

J essica wasn't sure what to expect from a ten-year-old girl's room, but whatever it was, she wasn't disappointed.

It was a mix of fairy tale decorations, movie posters, and paraphernalia.

The celebrity theme was more than obvious. Sophie loved the *Asterlight* movies even more than Jessica had already figured out. It was kind of awe-inspiring to see all the fan items displayed with such care in one place.

"Wow. This is cool." She glanced around, meaning it. She hadn't been one to hang posters on her wall, but she was suddenly seeing the allure of surrounding yourself with your heroes.

She turned and stopped. She was there, in her *Asterlight* gear, looking fierce and tough and powerful.

"I look so strong in that picture!" Had she ever been that strong in real life?

"You *are* strong," Sophie insisted.

"No, I just play a strong character." She couldn't seem to take her gaze off the picture of her. Had she never really looked at the promo shots? Maybe just long enough to give the minimal approval she was allowed back then.

But now she couldn't help but study them from an outside view. She did look strong. The woman on that poster could take on the world. Was that inside her somewhere, too?

"What's the difference?" Sophie asked.

"Well…" She thought through her answer as she climbed on Sophie's bed next to her. "Strong characters make a movie great. Strong people make the world great."

Sophie stared at her a long moment, as if this were a new idea that deserved her attention. Jess liked that about the girl. She didn't take anything at face value, always thinking things through and coming up with a smart conclusion.

"When I grow up, I want to be strong." After a moment, Sophie added, "And famous!"

Jessica thought about her life and suddenly wished for something different for Sophie. She loved it—she wouldn't trade it for anything… at least, she didn't think she would.

"Famous for what?" Because there were a lot of types of fame, and Jessica didn't want to sway her.

Sophie shrugged because, why think that far ahead? "Just for being me."

Jess was about to laugh this off, but then she remembered how old Sophie was… and YouTube.

"Well, luckily that's why they created the internet."

Sophie grinned and Jess could already see the wheels rolling.

"How did you become famous?" she asked.

"You mean, besides being an actress?"

"Yeah? Was it great?" Sophie asked.

"It was… and not. I started acting by accident in high school, and it was weird to not have my friends around all the time. I missed a lot. When I got to go home, it was like no one remembered I was one of them. My friends started forgetting about me—even when I was home."

"But you were famous," Sophie insisted.

"I was getting there, but that didn't mean that I got to have everything. I had the opportunity to do some things I wouldn't have otherwise, but"—Jessica brushed a lock of Sophie's hair out of her face as she watched her closely—"that doesn't mean I didn't miss out on stuff, too."

"Like Christmas stuff."

"Exactly, like Christmas stuff."

She thought about the Larsons and realized that Christmas stuff was more than just during Christmas. It was how they lived: family, tradition, friends.

A list that felt almost unreachable for her sometimes. But sitting there with Sophie, she felt more love than she'd felt in a long time.

"So, where are you going to spend Christmas this year?"

"At home in Los Angeles." She pressed back her disappointment again that Jill had canceled on her. Fiji with a girlfriend would have been just the break she needed after this.

"Why?" Sophie asked, sounding more confused than she had about any of the other things they'd discussed.

"Because that's where I live." Jess was glad Sophie was keeping to the simple questions, because if she circled back to inviting her to stay with them, Jessica was afraid she just might cave.

"That's not what you said."

Jessica looked up, confused by what Sophie was saying. Had she told her about going somewhere else and she'd assumed she lived there? Fiji was nice, but probably not a place she could live without getting antsy for more things to do. It was definitely relaxation central.

"What do you mean?" Jess asked.

"In *Asterlight: The Dragon's Lair*, you said, 'Home isn't where you live. It's where you love.'" Sophie smiled at her so sweetly it nearly broke Jessica's heart. "It was my mom's favorite of your movies, too."

Jess sucked in a breath, afraid to say the wrong thing and incredibly touched that one of her movies lived here, in this house, as a connection Sophie could have with her mom.

"It was?" She knew *The Dragon's Lair* was probably

a favorite for a lot of people. But hearing Sophie share that it was hers and her mom's was more personal than she expected.

"Uh-huh. She went to heaven when I was little, so I don't really remember, but Aunt Zoe told me that she really liked your movies." Sophie gave her a bright, trusting smile. "And now I do, too."

It was obvious that Sophie was looking for any connection she could find with her mom, that even the love of the same movies was a touchstone.

"You know…" Jess soft-stepped into her thought. "Just because people aren't around doesn't mean they aren't thinking about you."

Beside her, Sophie stilled, an action so out of character that Jessica nearly froze herself.

"Really?"

"Sure," she went on, desperately hoping she had the right thing to say in her somewhere. "Look at Santa Claus. He only comes around once a year. But the rest of the time, he's thinking about you and keeping track of whether you're naughty or nice."

"I'm nice!" Sophie insisted.

"Yes, you are." Jessica's heart melted. She was falling in love with this little girl far too quickly. "And he knows that. So when he comes on Christmas, he can bring you the perfect gift."

Sophie nodded. "Okay. That's cool."

"Do you know what you want for Christmas?"

"I think so." Sophie gave her a speculative look, and Jessica wondered if her trust was being measured.

"What?" Jessica was genuinely interested in what she might want. Besides a zebra.

"I can't tell you," Sophie said, although it felt like the *duh* was left silent. "Christmas wishes are just between you and Santa."

"Got it. You're absolutely right. Well, whatever it is, I'm sure you're going to get it."

Matt needed to go rescue Jessica. She'd been upstairs with Sophie for over twenty minutes. Not to mention, if he didn't get Sophie tucked in, she'd be a living terror in the morning, her typical drama-princess behavior morphing into something far more ugly.

He walked down the hall, catching their voices as he approached.

Sophie was, once again, talking about those movies she loved that Jessica was in. Then he heard her talking about her mom. Matt stalled out just as he had raised his hand to push the door open.

Sophie didn't ask about her mom very often. She'd asked a lot at certain times and then she'd stop asking. He and Zoe both made sure to mention Melanie whenever it made sense to keep a feel of her around for Sophie to relate to.

But hearing her talk to a stranger, to open her heart to Jessica, just blew him away.

Jessica filled the silence.

"You know..." Jessica's voice barely made it

through the door. "Just because people aren't around doesn't mean they aren't thinking about you."

He almost rushed in, but he was frozen in place, waiting to see how Jessica's thoughtful words would play out.

Sophie's equally soft reply came. "Really?"

"Sure. Look at Santa Claus. He only comes around once a year. But the rest of the time he's thinking about you and keeping track of whether you're naughty or nice."

Matt let his head fall softly against the door, taking a deep breath and sending up a prayer of thanks for this woman who came as a gift to his daughter at this time of the year.

He pushed the door open and stood, watching the woman wrap her arms around his daughter and her respond in kind. Clearing his throat, he stepped in, afraid he was intruding but still not able to retreat.

"Hey, what's going on in here?" Matt asked in the same teasing tone as if they might really be up to something when Sophie had a friend over.

"We were just talking about what Santa's going to bring me for Christmas." Sophie gave him a bright smile.

"I thought you said that was a secret." Matt glanced between them, not quite pulling off being hurt.

"Dad, it is a secret. I didn't tell Jessica." She grinned at her, too. "Sorry."

"No problem. I completely understand." Jess gave

her another squeeze. "Just promise your father it isn't a zebra so everyone can rest easy tonight."

He picked Sophie up, shaking her as she giggled, and announced it was time for bed. While he did, Jessica slipped out the door. This was where the friendship line ended.

She was pulling back behind that wall Rosalie had pointed out, and he couldn't help but wonder again if it really was for the best.

The next morning, Jessica was waiting for the shoot to start as she glanced around the set, catching glimpses of all the people who had become friends and neighbors.

She couldn't help the giggle she had to stifle as she caught a quick peek of Gavin and his mini-me, Sophie. Everything he did, she mimicked. When he finally gave her his attention, she flashed him that famous Larson smile.

That girl was going to be a heartbreaker.

Jess snatched her attention back in time to give her line. "I just wanted to let you know that I'm leaving tomorrow."

"Before Christmas? Why?" Vince—well, Vince's character—passed the question off with enough balance of sincerity and surprise.

"It's just gotten too..." Jessica forced herself not to glance toward Matt. "Everything was so easy before I got here."

"And now?" Vince's character prompted.

"Now?" She smiled a bit sadly, finding a new, stronger connection with her character. "Now it's complicated."

"It doesn't have to be. It really can be as simple as 'I love you.'"

Jessica gasped—well, her character did, but Jessica was a pro, so she felt it to her soul. "That's not simple at all."

She shook her head, not knowing what else to say. Realizing she didn't have to because that was her last line, she turned and ran out of the shot, stopping just at her end mark.

"And cut." Barbara walked into the scene, glancing around, taking all the details in from in front of the camera. "Great! I need one more shot here."

"Barbara, we don't have time to do any more tonight." Jessica ran the schedule through her head, searching for some empty space for whatever it was Barbara wanted to do. "We have to be out of here for the snowball fight."

"Snowball fight?" Barbara was obviously not down with that. "Jessica, we're already running behind. Can't they wait?"

Could they? The town might, but who knows? They might be getting sick of all their schedules getting shifted. And, for the first time in her career, it was incredibly easy to remember that they were actually guests here.

"No." She shook her head. "We promised. Look,

we've all been working like crazy. Let's take a break and blow off some steam. We'll figure out where we can shave off some time. Okay?"

"Okay," Barbara said, but that obviously wasn't how she was really feeling.

But, for once, Jessica knew that wasn't her problem. She wasn't the scout on this, and she hadn't picked the location. She doubted very much that they hadn't known what they were getting when they signed on. Heck, they'd told her about the grumpy mayor, so they'd definitely known.

Now, she was trying to adhere to what they'd agreed to, and she was the bad guy—or worse in actress-land—a diva.

She glanced around again, though, knowing she'd made the right decision. She wasn't running them through another broken promise if she could help it.

If Matt were writing this scene, he'd open it with evil laughter, because he was ready to do some snowball fighting damage.

Politely.

So no one got hurt.

It was all just fun and games.

But with evil laughter.

He was lined up, ready to rock, with Sophie and Zoe having his back. Jessica was there, too, but he doubted she had ever even made a snowball. Vince, on the other hand, was looking a little dangerous. And somehow, Jessica had talked Rosalie into showing up, too. Of course, Rosalie might just be keeping a watch on her charge. Matt shouldn't have been surprised with how seriously they took keeping Jessica safe, but still.

Which left Gavin, who was guarding the group of them... from a safe distance off to the side with Barbara, who was shouting into her phone, as usual.

Matt glanced to his side where Sophie stood, bouncing on her toes, ready to go, so glad that he didn't have a job that made him travel often without her. He couldn't imagine being away from home for long sweeps of time like the movie crew. How incredibly blessed was he to work from home so he could be there and not miss any of her growing-up years?

Between the rows of ready snow warriors, Pete paced, laying down the law.

"Okay, you know the rules. You can only use snow from the big pile. We've made sure that there are no rocks or anything else that could hurt anyone. And everyone has to wear their safety goggles!" Pete waved a pair to emphasize his point.

Pete stopped in front of their group as Jessica put hers on. She gave him a smile and a wave. Matt tried not to laugh because he was pretty sure Pete was trying not to stutter and drop dead on the spot.

"The rest is like dodgeball," Pete continued, hurrying on down the line. "Just try to avoid getting hit. If you do, you're out. The last team standing wins!

Got it? Okay... May the best team win in three, two, one... Snowball!"

Both teams rushed toward the pavilion tent in the center, grabbing the snow and few pre-made snowballs as quickly as they could and launching them at the other side.

There was barely-controlled pandemonium in the square as everyone had a blast scooping up snow, making snowballs, and throwing them while trying to dodge ones coming at them.

Matt couldn't believe Jessica had joined in. But there she was, right next to him, the Xena Warrior Princess of snowball fights. She dodged a ball then gave him a shove, making the snowball from Mr. Teatly, his minister, zip right past him.

He squashed the desire to high-five her.

They were invincible.

Then, it happened.

In slow motion, he saw Vince narrow in on him, ready to take him out. There was nothing he could do to get out of the way without trampling small children. A ball flew out of nowhere, striking Vince across the back and knocking him out before he could launch his weapon.

He glanced to his right, and Jessica stood there, tossing a spare ball in the air and giving him a wink.

And it was at that moment, over a snowball fight rescue, that he realized that Jessica McEllis was more of a danger to his heart than any snowball on the field was to the rest of him.

He watched as she turned toward her next victim. For some unknown reason, Barbara was standing in the middle of the crowd on the other team—on the phone.

As usual.

Jessica shaped up a new snowball and tossed it in the air as she pointed at Barbara.

She stopped and gave Jessica a hard stare. "Don't you dare."

In response, Jess tossed the snowball one more time and then winged it at her director, hitting her in the shoulder holding the phone up.

Matt laughed, realizing he would have taken the phone out completely if given the chance.

Barbara, very calmly, wiped off her phone and put it back to her ear. "Mommy has go hurt someone now."

Next to him, Jessica hid her laughter in her mittens. She elbowed Matt to make sure he was paying attention as he dodged another set of snow missiles to watch the Director Versus the Starlet showdown.

"Oh." Barbara nodded her head as if to say, It's on. "You've done it now."

Sophie gave a little squeal and ran to hide behind Gavin, using him as a human shield. The man didn't even flinch as Barbara scooped up snow and lifted it to throw.

They were officially sucked into the snowball war.

CHAPTER SIXTEEN

Zoe always loved the snowball fight—it was just competitive enough for her taste. But mostly good-natured. The perfect balance. Let Matt have the tree lighting; she'd take the snowball fight any holiday.

She'd actually tried to get an Easter Egg War going when she was a kid, but the parental units put a kibosh on that.

She glanced around, looking for Mike Monroe. She took him out every year since she'd asked him to be her boyfriend when she was seven and he told her she was smelly.

Every. Year. Like her own secret mission in life.

Before she could find him, she spotted Ian on the side of the crowd, a place she realized he lived, camera in hand.

This might be even better than Mike Monroe.

She headed his way, knowing she was going to nail him even though he wasn't officially in. Clearing her throat, she tossed her snowball in the air, making it obvious she was coming for him.

"Zoeeee," Ian warned. "No. This is a very expensive camera."

She shrugged and shook her head in mock sorrow. "You come to a snowball fight, you better expect to get hit."

With the talk over, she tossed the ball at him.

Ian—knowing it was coming—leapt to the right, successfully dodging her volley, only to go down hard in a pile of snow.

She was willing to call that a win.

"Why do I keep falling into snow?" Ian glanced around at the white stuff surrounding him as if he was surprised to find it there.

"Karma." Zoe shook her head. The snow always won. "That's why. Are you okay?"

"Great." Ian dusted himself off as he stood and smiled down at Zoe.

"Wait." She glanced to the side when a weird beep sounded from the snow. "Do you hear that?"

Ian checked his pockets then rolled his eyes heavenward as if asking the universe, *Why me?* "It's my phone. Where is it?"

She dug through the snow, following the beep until she saw a dim light shining through. She grabbed it and wiped it off as Ian dusted the snow from his legs. She was about to hand it back when the message on the screen hit home.

"I'm sorry. That was rude of me. I shouldn't have read that."

He glanced down at the message, knowing this wasn't going to end well. It was something that Zoe wouldn't be able to let go now that she'd read it, even if it were an accident.

"They are offering double for the picture of Jessica." Her head came up, gaze clashing with his. "What photo?"

"I haven't sold it," he defended.

Zoe knew it was even worse than she feared when he dodged the question.

"Okay. So what is it of?" she asked, more demanding this time but hoping that she was wrong. "What are they willing to double their offer for?"

Ian glanced away, running a hand across the back of his neck. His gaze slid over to the field of snowball warriors, landing on her family and staying there.

Her stomach dropped out.

"It's a picture of her kissing your brother," he admitted.

Zoe stopped and rethought what she was pretty sure he just said.

"Kissing? What are you talking about?" She gave an awkward laugh, trying to play it off. Zoe couldn't believe he was making this up. Her brother would not get involved with someone who was leaving in a few days. "No, wait. He didn't kiss her."

Ian shook his head as if there was nothing he could do about it. "I've got the picture to prove it."

He was obviously annoyed she didn't believe him.

But annoyed or not, once he started talking about the picture, Zoe's brain went into overdrive, realizing all the implications of that picture getting out.

"Ian, you can't sell that." It seemed so obvious. Why were they even discussing this?

"We're talking about a lot of money, Zoe." He glanced away and back again. "A lot."

"And we're talking about my brother's life." The heat of anger rushed up her neck, making the three layers she was wearing redundant. "He has a ten-year-old daughter. Do you know what those stupid tabloids write about people? What they'll do to them?"

He shook his head, finally not able to face her.

"Hey, please tell me you won't sell that picture. Please."

Ian paused, obviously torn. Zoe didn't know what she'd do if he didn't agree. How could she protect Matt from this?

The fact that this could change everything ran through her head over and over.

Matt was far too naïve to see what this would mean. He saw the best, the simplest, the happiest in everyone. She'd have to take care of this herself if Ian didn't agree.

Ian must have read the resolve on her face because he sagged a bit.

"Okay," Ian caved but didn't sound remotely happy about it.

"Just, okay?" She pushed, afraid he was humoring her.

"Yeah." He shook his head, as if giving up a fight she didn't know he was having. "Okay."

"Thank you." She reached out and took his hand, giving it a squeeze.

The relief that rushed through her was insane. She loved her brother, and while he might not see it this way, she was incredibly protective of him since he'd lost Melanie. This picture being shared with the world—it was so not going to happen.

As she walked away, she glanced over her shoulder and pointed at a snow pile. "Watch your step. Karma."

Matt glanced down at his daughter, who was looking particularly smug since she was the winner of the snowball war. Of course, it had come down to her or Jessica, and no one wanted to hit the movie star... except for Sophie.

"I can't believe you turned on your own dad."

"You said, 'go,'" Sophie insisted.

"I said, 'no. No! Noooo.'"

But Jessica had laughed so hard, he'd thought it was worth it all around.

"Gavin, will you take them to the car? I'll be there in a minute. I just have to grab my notes from the trailer." Jessica headed off to probably wrap up some movie stuff as Gavin steered them through the remainder of the crowd with Sophie walking ahead. She obviously had no idea where she was going, but the way Sophie charged forward, she'd get there pretty darn quickly.

Sophie laughed at him as he reenacted his death by snowball in slow motion.

As he hit his chest with an imaginary snowball, he felt Jessica's phone in his coat pocket from when she'd asked him to hold it during the snowball fight.

If she was finishing work stuff, she might need something on her calendar or whatever fancy Hollywood apps she was running.

He turned to Gavin. "I have Jessica's phone. I'll be right back."

As he walked away, he heard his daughter squeak up at the bodyguard. "So exactly how tall are you?"

Matt almost went back to rescue Gavin but figured if the man could dodge bullets, he could handle a ten-year-old.

Probably.

But then, he heard him answer, "Tall," and figured no one would need to dodge a bullet.

Jessica couldn't believe the night she'd just had. If she'd been told even two weeks ago she'd be in a small town in the middle of frozen, wintery Iowa having a snowball fight, she would never have believed it.

But now... she'd had so much fun. Who would

have guessed? And, she was even getting used to the cold. Not used to it as in, enjoying it, but she didn't feel like crying each time she left a building now.

She reached for her trailer door, happy to get out of that not-quite-as-hated cold, when she heard her name.

"Jessica!" She turned to see Vince hurrying after her. "Jess, wait a minute…"

He was not the person she was most excited to see. She wasn't sure what was up with him, but it was definitely not cool. Not only was he making the film shoot feel weird, but he was putting Matt on guard, which was the last thing she needed.

Now, when it was just the two of them, was the perfect time to figure it out. Starting with the snowball fight tonight. It was all good fun, but the look on Vince's face when he'd turned on Matt said *Seek and Destroy*, not *Good Time Dodgeball*.

Vince shook his head and smiled, as if this weren't an issue. Instead, he took her hand and stopped her outside her trailer.

"I'm not acting."

"You're not…" Jessica didn't know where this was going. Did he mean he wasn't acting tomorrow? That he wasn't showing up to set? "I'm sorry, you're not what?"

"In our scenes," he rushed on. "When my character says how all these old feelings are stirring up. When he says how much she means to him. When he says, 'I love you'… I'm not acting."

She wasn't sure how to address what he'd just said. He was a dear friend, someone she'd always value and want in her life. But she knew now, no matter what, he wasn't The Guy.

Sure, actors got sucked into their roles, but she'd never expected it of Vince.

"Oh, Vince..."

"I know I said we'd keep it professional, but..." He took both her hands in his, leaning down to look at her eye to eye. "Just give me one more chance."

She shook her head, her heart breaking to have to say this. "Vince, I can't."

He let go of her hand, shifting back and away from her, his disappointment obvious.

"Why? Is it because of Mayor Matty?"

She'd figured out that love was an uncontrollable thing. And she didn't feel that kind of love for Vince. Her feelings, or lack thereof, didn't reflect on Vince—and when Vince learned that lesson for himself, he'd have found the woman for him.

"No, it has nothing to do with him."

"But you care about him, right?" He paused and then pushed on. "I mean, it's pretty obvious."

It was? She still didn't know what she felt.

"I don't..." She stopped, a rush of frustration and confusion overtaking her. "Vince, I have to go. I'm sorry. Let's talk tomorrow, okay?"

He nodded, obviously wanting the moment to be over, as she rushed away.

She hurried into her trailer, closing the door

behind her with a definitive *click*. She couldn't deal with this right now. There were too many other things going on to manage Vince and Matt.

Contrary to what the tabloids said, her life was more than what guy she was dating.

She glanced out the window as Vince walked away, wishing that it was just that simple and doubting it would be.

CHAPTER SEVENTEEN

"I'm not acting." Vince's voice drifted around the corner, stopping Matt in his tracks.

Matt froze, eavesdropping when he knew better. If he caught Sophie doing this, they'd have some serious words.

"You're not... What?"

"In our scenes. When my character says how all these old feelings are stirring up. When he says how much she means to him. When he says, 'I love you'... I'm not acting."

"Oh, Vince..." Jessica's voice came back, and Matt knew there was no sense sticking around.

He split before she could tell Vince that she loved him, too. The last thing he needed was to hear her undying love for Vince and a make-up, make-out session.

Instead, he picked up Sophie from Gavin and took

her straight home. She was upstairs getting her reading time after he'd tucked her in, and he sat in the lodge's sitting room, picking a cherry pie apart.

He was enjoying a perfectly good brood when Zoe came in and joined him.

"Mmm, pie." Zoe plopped down next to him and took a swipe at his fork. "Yes, please."

He gave up on his fork and pushed the rest of his plate toward her. "It's all yours."

Zoe went to dig in, then paused. "Are you all right?"

Matt played with his coffee cup, not wanting to get into this, even with his sister—maybe especially with his sister.

"It's nothing. It's dumb." He thought through the whole thing and added, "I'm dumb."

"Well, yes." She nodded as if this were the most obvious thing in the world. "Most big brothers are."

Oh, Zoe. She was exactly what he needed. Without knowing it, he smiled, feeling himself lighten up just a bit.

"What, specifically, are you being dumb about?" She took a huge bite of the pie he was starting to regret giving to her.

Was this something he wanted to say out loud? Then, thinking about her, he just said it... no taking it back. "Jessica."

"Jessica?" Zoe said in a super-neutral voice. "As in, you and Jessica?"

Yeah, it did sound stupid when he said it out loud. "Surprised?"

"Not as much as you may think."

He had no idea what that meant, but he figured he'd keep going. He was in this deep. He might as well just run through the whole darn thing.

"I thought there was something there. For the first time since Melanie died..." He paused, choking up like he always did over his wife's name. "But it's crazy, and now there's Vince, and I can't compete with that. And even if there wasn't Vince, I still don't know how she could ever..."

These were almost insurmountable problems even if Jessica did feel the same way about him. He looked at Zoe, trying to read the expression on her face.

"What do I do?" he asked, genuinely wanting and trusting her feedback.

She reached over and took his hand. "Be careful."

Well... that wasn't what he expected.

"What do you mean?" It wasn't like Jessica was going to pull out a real sword on him and go all *Asterlight* girl.

"They don't call them stars for nothing. People like her have their own gravitational pull. It's easy to get caught up in that. But then you and all the other people in her sphere have to deal with everything else in her orbit."

She made a motion with her hands to simulate a planetary orbit. Which was so weird that Matt considered asking her if she was including Pluto.

"Zoe. I get it, it's just…" Matt shook his head, not really sure where to even start. "That was a terrible metaphor."

"That was a great metaphor! Stars. Movie stars! Come on!"

No. He shook his head. Just no. "Give me back the pie."

"No. Not after that." She pulled the pie closer. "Get your own!"

"That is mine, pre-ridiculous metaphor."

"Possession is nine-tenths the law." She shoved more pie into her mouth, one less bite he could try to get back.

"What does that even mean?"

"I don't know. I just know I'm in possession of the pie, and if you touch it, I'll call the law."

The front door opened and closed, a rush of wind chasing Jessica into the hall.

"Hey." Jessica poked her head into the room, ending the bickering abruptly.

"Oh, hey. Hi." Matt let go of the pie and leaned back.

"Sorry to interrupt, I just…" She looked around as if wondering how she'd gotten there. "Gavin said you have my phone?"

"Oh right." Obviously, she wanted her phone. And, obviously, he was an idiot. "Yes, it's over in my place. Do you want to follow me over and I'll grab it?"

He nodded his head toward the Larsons' part of the lodge so she knew what he meant.

"Sure, that would be great."

He rose, ignoring the look Zoe gave him as he did.

He hefted his coffee then realized Jessica had just come in from outside. "Would you like a cup of coffee?"

"Oh yes, please." She sounded like he'd offered her polished diamonds, not heated water.

He picked out a cup and poured her the coffee, adding a little cream like he'd seen her do, as she wished Zoe good night.

Matt gave Zoe a look as she sat eating his pie and watching them go. She didn't say anything, but he heard the echo of her words earlier.

He followed Jessica outside, accepting the distance she put between them when she made it clear she'd wait on the porch as he ran into his quarters to fetch her phone. He expected to give it to her and head back inside for some additional pie therapy. Instead, he stopped at the railing beside her, both of them letting the coffee mugs warm their hands.

"Thanks." She took it as if he'd given her something valuable, something definable, something more than a phone.

"Of course."

Zoe had mentioned she probably had a bazillion famous people on her phone. He hadn't been tempted to look, but after watching the paparazzi follow her around, he'd hate to be responsible for anything personal falling into their hands. He thought of the pictures he had of Sophie on his and was glad Jessica's was back in her possession.

They looked out at the lights of the town. No matter how many Christmases he lived here, he'd never tire of this—of the beauty, the peace, the white lights on snow, the sense of belonging and community they gave him every year.

As if to echo his thoughts, Jessica spoke into the quiet.

"It's so beautiful here." Her words sat out there, showing how strongly in accord they were, then she added, "I could get used to this."

"Really?" He heard the hope in his voice and tried to squash it.

She had to mean quiet moments—not the holidays in Homestead with him.

"Sure." Jessica turned, angling her body to lean against the railing and face him. "I mean, it's nice being out of the spotlight for a change."

Matt looked at her in disbelief. It was amazing how different her view of the world was than—well, almost everyone else's. He couldn't help it when the laugh slipped out.

"Sorry." He waved a hand at her to give him a moment as he pulled it together. "You have an entire movie crew, paparazzi, and a bodyguard following you around all day, every day. That's the very definition of the spotlight."

He felt a little bad when she gave him a sheepish smile.

"Okay. Fair enough." She glanced side-to-side as if to prove a point. "None of that is around now…"

He knew it wasn't as simple as that. He couldn't forget what he'd just seen. "What about Vince?"

Jessica stopped, taken by surprise by this question. "What about him?"

"He's still in love with you."

She nodded slowly. It was clear she wasn't going to deny it. "Yes. And I still love him. But I'm not *in* love with him anymore."

"Are you sure?" He found it hard to believe that. "Because that's some pretty stiff competition. I got nothing on that."

"No." Her smile softened as she glanced away. "It's not even close."

Her gaze came back to his, and she leaned in, obviously welcoming his kiss. But just at the last moment, Matt pulled back.

"I'm sorry." He ran a hand through his hair, upset as well as annoyed, trying to rein in all the emotions he hadn't felt in years flooding him. "We shouldn't."

She stopped, looking flustered and beautiful.

Matt struggled to find something—anything—to say.

"No, it's okay," she answered, obviously not okay with it at all. "I understand."

He was being even more stupid than normal.

"Look, you're leaving in a few days," he explained. He took another small step back, more like shifting his weight, just enough to give him a little distance, a little breathing room.

She sucked in a breath, sounding desperate as she hadn't before. "What if I don't?"

"Don't what?" Matt didn't know if he should be hopeful or confused. "Don't leave?"

"Yes." She faced him full-on, tacking on to her thought. "Maybe I should take Sophie up on her offer and stay for Christmas. See that Festival of Lights you mentioned?"

For a moment, Matt's heart actually stopped beating. She was offering to stay here with him and Sophie. But then he realized the whole picture. He had to be a mature adult here, not a man reaching for what he wanted. He had to think of not only protecting his own heart, but Sophie's, as well.

"Christmas ends. Even here in Homestead. What then?" He smiled at her, trying to make her understand he didn't want to say no. "You may not think there's a spotlight on you here, but there is. It was made for you. It just wasn't made for me."

Jessica took half a step back, smiling at him sadly. Then she placed a hand softly on his cheek and leaned in to kiss the other. Before he could find more words, she turned and walked away, leaving Matt to question his sanity.

Ian was feeling pretty good about everything. This

trip to Homestead, Iowa—of all places—was an eye-opening surprise. And so was Zoe.

He kept walking, thinking about Zoe and how she had him rethinking what he was doing and why. And the possibility of something better.

Getting out would be hard. What else could he do? It wasn't the mafia, for goodness' sake.

But the bitter taste in his mouth every time he sold a photo would only be worse after seeing his world through Zoe's eyes. He couldn't help but wonder how many other families had been impacted by a picture he'd taken... and actually shared.

But he was a good photographer. The paparazzi didn't take photos; they took snapshots—millions of them—and hoped for the best. The one that would bring them a big payoff.

With only Jessica and Vince to follow—and to be honest, Vince wasn't as big of a draw, since people wanted women messing up, not men—Ian had the freedom to shoot other things. The town lit up, the blur of a speeding snowball, the trees with the moon showing through them.

Zoe.

It made him remember why he'd picked up a camera in the first place.

Maybe, just maybe, he could make a go of it without losing his soul after all.

His phone rang and the bells felt like ringing in a new life.

"Hello?"

"Ian, Mickey."

Great, business call. He'd rather be Christmas shopping.

"Mickey, what's up?"

"I'm just letting you know, I got even more for that Jessica McEllis picture than I told you I would. Son, you are basically set for life. Shame they weren't naked, but this was enough after her years with Vince—not to mention Vince is up there with her—to get you a nice paycheck."

"You did what? Mickey, no!" Ian couldn't even hear the numbers Mickey was throwing out. All he could hear was his promise to Zoe. "I said don't sell the picture!"

"Too late, son. It's not only sold, but it's live. And viral."

"No." Ian shook his head. "I gotta go."

Those dreams were going away quickly. He'd finally gotten what he wanted, a viral paparazzi shot, and realized that he'd always be that guy. Not many paparazzi were able to be taken seriously after making a name for themselves as a money chaser.

He doubted he'd be any different.

And he definitely didn't know how he was going to face Zoe.

CHAPTER EIGHTEEN

J essica was trying to put on a happy face. Last
night was—not what she'd expected. She'd gone
to bed after going through more emotions in one day
than she'd thought was possible. Turning down Vince,
coming on to Matt, getting turned down by Matt,
realizing that her dream job was costing her something
she didn't know she'd wanted this badly.

Something she suspected wasn't part of her future
with the path she'd chosen.

But the day was new, and she had to do her best
to make this movie come together and be a success.
That's what she was here for. It was time to put all
these emotions aside and do her job. Refocus on how
badly she'd wanted this producer role before all these
guys started getting involved.

She was just taking a deep, centering breath when
there was a rapid, hard knock on her door.

"Jessica!" Rosalie's voice rushed through in. "Jessica, open up!"

She hurried to the door, pulling it mostly open before Rosalie rushed in, slamming it behind her.

"What is going on?"

"This." She waved her tablet around. "You kissed him?"

It took her a moment to realize what she was asking, but her panic was over *who* they assumed she was kissing. "No. I absolutely didn't kiss him."

Rosalie shoved the tablet at her. Jess glanced down, shocked to see a picture of her and Matt in her trailer looking like they were kissing. Jessica was pretty darn sure she'd remember kissing Matt. Especially since she'd made an attempt last night and been shot down.

But there it was. In vivid color on Rosalie's tablet with the headline, *Jessica's New Small-Town Flame.*

And, of course, it had gone viral, so there were further lines like, JMac Caught Kissing New Guy! and JMac Dates Innkeeper on Screen and in Real Life.

How could this occur?

Nothing had happened between them. One of the reasons for that was to avoid exactly this scenario. But now, here it was, about to ruin Matt's life and put his ability to keep Sophie safe in the privacy of their home at risk. This changed everything.

It was like gaining the weight without getting the cupcakes.

There were going to be paparazzi everywhere.

She had to warn him. She had to make sure they were ready for what was coming.

Jessica tossed Rosalie's tablet on the bed and rushed out the door, hoping she could make this right.

He was going to act like everything was normal. Totally normal. Not at all like he'd turned down a movie star who just happened to be the first woman he had feelings for since he'd lost his wife.

He'd treat her the same as he had the whole time.

Well, maybe not the whole time—he had been a bit grumpy when she'd arrived.

But like friends. They were friends—at least, he hoped they were.

His phone buzzed, and he figured that was enough thinking about girls and emotions and stuff. Saved by the bell and all that.

"Hello?"

"Is this Ma—arson?"

"Yes." What a cruddy connection. Must be a snowstorm coming in.

"D—" Static filled the line until the last word came through. "—picture?"

Zoe and Sophie came running in the front door with confused, worried looks on their faces. But he could only deal with one event at a time. First, figure out this phone call and if they needed to batten down for a storm.

"Matt!" Zoe waved her hand at him, trying to get his attention away from the call.

He held up the phone and gave her a look. She knew better than to interrupt when he was on the business line. She'd kill him if he did that to her.

"Hello? Sorry, who's this? It's a bad connection."

"Do—comment—picture?" the voice said.

"The picture? What picture? I'm sorry, what?"

"Matt!" Zoe waved again, all but taking the phone from him.

"Shhh." He put his finger to his lips. "I'm going to step outside to see if the reception is any better."

"Matt! Matt!" Jessica rushed at him down the stairs, but he couldn't deal with her right now. The phone call was a great excuse. He gave her a quick wave and opened the front door.

From behind him, he heard a desperate, "No!" and was distracted for a moment. And then, because who could help but notice it, he became aware of the huge group of photographers on his front lawn.

It was complete chaos in front of the lodge. People shouting at him—so many at a time he couldn't understand even one of them. Then the flashes started to go off, one after another, blinding him.

Before he could figure out what to do, Sophie and Zoe rushed out behind him, stopping on the top stair and glancing from him to the mass. And that was when things got crazy.

The light bulbs flashed so fast he wondered how they got any pictures. They all stood there dumbfounded until Sophie, realizing this was her big chance at fame, started posing for the camera.

Matt's fatherly instincts kicked in. He tossed her up into his arms and carried her into the house as she waved at the paparazzi over his shoulder, obviously not bothered one bit by their invasion of privacy.

Matt was bothered.

Matt was *very* bothered.

And he was about five minutes away from losing his cool if he didn't find out exactly what was going on.

He headed to the person he was pretty sure was responsible. She better have some answers—the right ones—when he got there.

Jessica couldn't believe this was happening. It was bad enough that all of Hollywood had followed her to Homestead just as she was letting her guard down. But it was so very much worse now that it was impacting the Larsons.

Okay, so maybe Sophie was loving it, but still. She just didn't understand it was affecting her.

And that made Jessica even angrier.

Jessica and Rosalie were huddled in her room, trying to figure out how to handle this new crisis.

"Are you falling for this guy?" Rosalie asked.

"It doesn't matter if I am or not." She could hear the pout in her voice. She could not believe she was brooding over a guy. What was she, fifteen? "He's not falling for me."

Rosalie looked at her like she was an idiot. She always did give Jess too much credit for the movie-star stuff. She probably figured this was just an auto-yes situation since Jessica had the whole fame-and-fortune thing going on.

"How do you know that?" she asked.

Jessica could feel the heat coming to her face. What a humiliating moment. Not exactly one she wanted to relive.

"Because I offered to stay."

Rosalie was stunned silent for a moment—which was a first. Did everyone think it was a bad idea except for her? Now Jessica felt even weirder about the whole thing.

"Stay?" Rosalie's tone matched her shocked expression. "Here? Like forever?"

"No! Not..." She realized that everyone went to "forever" whenever she talked about staying. Was she the only person who thought short-term was okay? "I thought for Christmas. It was stupid."

Rosalie came to sit beside her on the bed, a casualness between them that had been missing for a while.

"Look, Jess, I get it." She wrapped an arm around her, giving her a tentative squeeze. "You're stressed out about the movie and Vince, and suddenly, you have this warm and fuzzy Christmas story come to life with the beautiful family and the carriage rides and—"

"You're worried about my career." She could hear the accusation in her voice.

But the truth was, how often did she get advice that was just "what's best for Jessica?" Anyone she trusted inside her life had some type of foothold in her world. Their own income and success and life hinged on what went on in hers. To pretend that she could blindly take advice from anyone was naïve—even if she wished it were true.

And then there'd been Matt.

Matt had made the hard decision for both of them because he thought it was what was best.

She hadn't realized how valuable that was last night around her embarrassment and disappointment, but now she did, and it made her like him even more.

"No," Rosalie insisted. "I'm worried about my friend. Give it all up and go live on a mountain and raise goats. I don't care as long as you're happy. But the story of the famous actress finding true love at Christmas in a small town? That's the plot of your movie. Not real life."

Sincerity rolled off her, buffeting Jess with a surety of her support that she hadn't realized she'd needed so desperately right then.

"So what do I do? Go back to L.A.?" That made sense. "Go back to Vince?"

"Oh, no! No!" Rosalie shook her head in emphasis. "Do that and *I* will give it all up and go raise goats."

She couldn't help but roll her eyes at that. Rosalie

was having a rough enough time being in a well-situated small town. Throw goats in, and she'd go nuts.

After a moment, Jessica admitted what the worst part of all this was. "I really do like him."

She waited for Rosalie's words of wisdom, but all she got was, "Matt, right? You like Matt?"

Oh for the love of hearts everywhere. "Yes!"

"Okay." She smiled apologetically and shrugged. "Just checking."

Jessica stared out the window, watching a light fall of snow drift down and thinking that no one got everything they wanted. With the life she had, she'd gotten so much, but was it really wrong to want one more thing?

With a sigh, she couldn't help but wonder if the answer was maybe.

This was exactly what he didn't want. Of course, Matt hadn't considered this a possibility, but fame wasn't something he'd ever aspired to. And not needing to be in the spotlight made him incredibly good at both of his jobs. He liked helping, not being out front.

And now there were at least two dozen people outside his home trying to get a picture of him.

How were he and Zoe going to handle this new and weird situation when the film crew left in a few days and they had new guests coming in? None of those people would want their privacy invaded like that. Not exactly the small-town, relaxing getaway Homestead Lodge advertised.

"What am I going to do?" He paced past Zoe for the one-hundredth time. "What is the town going to think? What are Mom and Dad going to think?"

Zoe swung her feet, sitting on the counter, looking for the life of her like she was a teenager watching her parents unravel at some silly rebellion.

"Of you kissing a movie star?" she asked like it was an everyday occurrence. "Oh my gosh. They're probably already having it made into Christmas cards."

He stopped, gave her a look, and then started pacing again because even though it didn't accomplish anything, it was doing something, and he desperately needed to be doing something.

"This is what you warned me about." He pointed at her. This was her fault. "The star's gravitational pull."

"I thought you hated that metaphor."

"Well." He glared at her, not happy with having his words thrown back at him. "It makes more sense now."

"Okay, look, maybe it's not so bad. I mean, the phones have been ringing off the hook with people wanting to stay here since this came out. Maybe this is what launches our franchise idea."

He skidded to a halt. His life was in a state of disarray so far from normal he barely recognized it. He'd had to cancel a play date for Sophie today, and he'd insisted she stay away from the windows—locked inside, like a mini, nicely-decorated prison.

And Zoe was bringing up the fact that she wanted a franchise. Right now.

"Zoe, enough with the franchise stuff." And then, because he was really ticked off and hurt she wanted to do this now, he added, "It's not going to happen."

Not that that made her back down.

"Why not?"

"Because we're a family-run lodge. That's what we have always been."

"It doesn't mean we can't be something else," Zoe insisted.

"I hate change, remember?" Was it selfish that he wanted this moment in time to be only about his breakdown?

There were like seven billion reporters outside. They were under siege, for goodness' sake!

Not that anyone but him seemed to notice.

Zoe studied him for a long, drawn-out moment.

"Matt, you know, when we were kids, I always found the Christmas presents you hid before you wrapped them."

He was too annoyed by the statement to wonder what the heck was going on with the super-powered change of subject.

"No, you did not."

"Really? Because the super cute watch under the tree over there begs to differ."

He had worked his tail off to come up with

something she needed, she'd like, and she'd be surprised by.

"Are you kidding me?"

"The point is that you and I both like to know what's coming next. And I get it." She gave him a look of such sympathy that he couldn't meet her gaze. "The difference is you want it to be the same thing over and over again. Can you imagine if you got the same Christmas present every year?"

Well, he had to agree with that—even if he did give great presents.

Before he could try to argue that she was using horrible metaphors again, there was a knock at the family door. He couldn't help but fear the reporters were getting more daring. The sheriff had set up some very clear parameters of what got trespassers thrown in jail here, but this group seemed desperate to one-up Ian's photograph.

He went to the door, peeking out to spot Gavin standing at his usual hyper-aware stance, guarding all the occupants.

When he saw who it was, Matt opened the door but couldn't help glancing past him and asking, "Are you with Jessica?"

Gavin—that chatty guy—just shook his head.

"Is she okay?"

A nod from Mr. Chatty.

"Can I help you?" Matt finally asked, beginning to wonder if he should break out their Pictionary drawing board.

"She wanted me to check on you…" He paused and glanced toward the stairs. "And your daughter."

"Sophie?" Matt shook his head, a bit surprised Gavin was asking about her with everything going on. Matt had kept her out of the spotlight, and that was all he really cared about. "She's fine. I'm the one who wants to hide under my bed."

Gavin nodded again, and Matt feared he was going to have to start guessing Gavin's part of the conversation again.

"That's a valid reaction," Gavin surprised him by saying. "But you're sure she's okay?"

"I think so." Actually, knowing his daughter, he was surprised she hadn't set up a hot chocolate stand outside or some other complex plan for her age. "Do you want to say hi?"

When Gavin nodded again, Matt stepped aside so he could come in and then shut the door behind him.

"Hey, Gavin." Zoe stood up, probably looking for an escape from their earlier conversation, and motioned toward the hall. "Her room's this way."

Gavin gave another one of his all-encompassing nods and followed Zoe down the hall toward the only person not worried about the new events of their very untraditional Christmas.

CHAPTER NINETEEN

Sophie was not thrilled about the fact that the reporters were neglecting to not only cover the most interesting things about her—but to cover her at all. There hadn't been one story about her, and she'd been looking.

What good was this going to do her against Hailey Shephard? She'd thought this would definitely beat having a horse any day, but getting ignored was not what she'd expected.

When a knock sounded on her door, she hoped for a moment that her dad was going to ask her about an interview. But it was just Aunt Zoe.

"Soph?" She stuck her head in, probably checking on her like they'd both been doing all day. "You have a visitor."

Before she could ask who, Aunt Zoe stepped aside so she could see Gavin filling the doorway.

"Hi, Gavin!" Sophie jumped up, excited to see her

soon-to-be bodyguard, if she could convince him to stick around. "Come on in."

Gavin stepped inside, and Zoe reached to close the door as she told them, "Have fun."

Sophie wasn't used to having grown-up guests. This was pretty neat. She settled back down at her tea-time table and waved her hand at the little chair across from her.

"Have a seat."

Gavin glanced around at her room and looked like a giant in tiny-furniture land. He pulled out the petite seat across from her and settled in, his knees coming almost as high as his chest.

"I've been looking, but they haven't posted any pictures of me yet."

She glanced at her tablet again, wondering why.

"You want them to post pictures of you?"

She couldn't believe he was asking that because... of course. "Doesn't everybody?" Fame seemed like a good thing—it meant everyone knew who you were and loved you.

"No," he answered, his tone making it clear that this was a certainty.

What? That made no sense.

"Why not?"

Gavin thought for a moment, letting her wonder exactly what it was she supposedly didn't know that adults did.

"Because some people like to keep their private lives private."

That didn't make any sense. Everyone in Homestead knew everything about her. She could barely have a secret here. And she should know. She'd told her best friend Hailey that Hailey Shephard was copying her hair ribbons. Ashley Promer heard them, and next thing she knew, everyone knew.

"I don't understand."

Gavin nodded as if he was taking her very seriously. She appreciated that. Lots of adults didn't bother to really listen to her.

After a second, he asked, "Why do you think Jessica needs me? A bodyguard?"

Well, that one was easy. "Because she's a movie star."

He nodded, but said, "No."

Because... adults. Geez.

Gavin gave her a very serious look she was sure he used on potential bad guys and went on. "Because she's a person. Just like you and me. And sometimes, she wants to do regular person stuff."

They'd been doing regular people stuff all week.

"Like what?" Because they'd gone skating, on the carriage ride, to the snowball fight, had hot chocolate, and she'd hung out with her in Sophie's room. She'd done all the regular people stuff.

"Like..." Gavin stopped and thought about it. "Going to the store to get Christmas presents. Or..."

That was one of the things Sophie was thinking about!

"And," she added, "like the Christmas parade? She was going to go with us tonight!"

Gavin shook his head. "I don't think she can do that now."

Sophie gave him a sad, confused look. "That's not fair."

"No, it's not." He shook his head. He'd probably seen Jessica have to miss a lot of stuff like that. "You get a lot, being famous. But you lose a lot, too."

She thought about this, annoyed that famous people didn't get to have the life she thought they did.

"But bodyguards are with you always, and they watch out for you. So they're like your best friend, right?"

She was pretty sure her best friend wasn't able to be her bodyguard.

Gavin gave her one of those adult smiles and nodded. "Right."

This was some serious stuff. She hadn't realized how big of a deal Jessica needing Gavin was.

"Well, I know I was trying to get you to come be my bodyguard, but you should stay with Jessica." She thought it through one more time, then went on. "She needs you more than I do."

"Yeah." Gavin nodded his head, but she could totally tell he was disappointed. "I think you might be right. But if you ever need help... You call me, okay? I'll give your Aunt Zoe my number."

She thought about it. Jessica did need Gavin more, and this was kind of like having a bodyguard on call.

"Okay." She offered him her hand to seal the deal. Once they were done with the business, she was able to be the hostess—just like her Aunt Zoe always was.

She handed him one of her little teacups. "Tea?"

"Absolutely."

She poured him some special tea from her little pot. "Pinkies out."

"Pinkies out." He nodded and took a sip, not pointing out the tea wasn't real like some grown-ups do. "Mmm… that's good."

"Do you want to see my stuffed animal collection?"

Gavin nodded seriously. She liked that about him. He knew what was important.

She grabbed her favorites because she knew he'd appreciate them.

Errands had to be run, but Matt wasn't loving being the one to run them. Especially with an audience. Who in their right mind would actually care what kind of nutmeg he bought for the holiday drinks? Rushing up the stairs, he hurried through the front door, slammed it behind him, and let his head fall back against it.

"Matt." He opened his eyes to see Jessica coming down the stairs. "I am *so* sorry."

"It's not your fault."

"A thousand photographers in your driveway?" She cocked an eyebrow at him in challenge. "That is the *definition* of my fault."

He didn't want to blame her, and he didn't want

her blaming herself. But he was feeling better about his decision last night. She wasn't staying, and the added attention if she had—even just for Christmas—would have been more than he could have handled.

"I guess the spotlight found us." He gave her a sad smile.

Jessica wasn't having it, though.

"I'm going to fix this. I don't know how, but..." She shook her head at him, and the resolve that came into her eyes nearly had him believing she could. "Maybe some other celebrity will do something dumb and it'll take the pressure off."

"We can always hope." Not that Matt found that in the least bit hopeful or comforting.

"It's only for a couple more days." She gave him a look that he tried to read, something between sad and resigned. "Then we'll be gone, and we can all get back to normal."

A curse and a blessing. Matt didn't know how to respond to that. He needed her to go, but he really wanted her to stay.

"Yeah." Sure, he was agreeing with her, but maybe he was really questioning it for the first time—maybe ever. "Normal is good."

She cleared her throat and glanced away, obviously awkward in this non-goodbye goodbye.

"I better..." She gestured vaguely in the opposite direction. "I've got to go to work."

"Okay. Yeah. Me, too." Matt pointed in a vague

swoop of the room because... well, he was already *at* work.

And he'd really like to stop saying stupid things about now.

"Okay."

She pivoted on the step, started to head up the stairs but then stopped.

"Have you seen Gavin around?"

"He's having a tea party with my daughter and her stuffed animals." Because today couldn't get much weirder, right?

Jessica smiled. "Maybe I was a little hasty on that getting-back-to-normal thing."

She finished her climb, leaving Matt watching her go... again.

How can they still be here? Zoe glanced across the street at the paparazzi as she headed along the deck to the other end of the lodge. What did they really expect to happen here?

"Zoe!"

Ian. Not worth her time. Nope. She didn't have time for lying liars.

"Zoe!"

Fine, he wanted to do this here and now?

She spun on him, surprising Ian into stopping in his tracks.

"You promised."

He nodded, agreeing with her as if that would make it better. As if it would help her brother—her adorable, idiot brother who was just coming out of his shell of no-change, no-risk after years of grief and emotional lockdown.

"I didn't do it." Ian hurried on as she shook her head and turned to go. "My agent, Mickey, did it. I didn't tell him to release the photos, I swear!"

She wanted to take him at his word, she really did. But she'd seen what happened when the photo went live. She could only imagine what he'd made off of it. It was what he did. A vulture. She'd known that, and yet, she'd felt bad for him.

Not anymore.

"I don't believe you."

His arm shot out, which she easily dodged.

"Zoe, listen..."

This wasn't a game. He didn't seem to realize that. And just like so many people, he'd underestimated her. Took her kindness for weakness. Well, she was not weak, and Matt and Sophie were the most important things in the world to her.

"Get off our property, or this time, I really will call the sheriff."

She went into their rear quarters and slammed the door, leaving that lying vulture out in the cold—not just literally.

CHAPTER TWENTY

B eauty sleep was not in Jess's near future, and with her job, she certainly should be getting some.

She glanced at the other two exhausted women looking at her over the table filled with timelines.

"Let's go through it again." There had to be something somewhere they'd missed.

"Jessica." Rosalie held up her iPad to clearly show the time. "It's three in the morning."

They'd had worse nights. And this was important.

"We have to figure this out," Jessica insisted.

"I'm telling you, we're not going to be able to get it done in two days." Barbara pointed to a sheet of paper filled with so many notes Jess wasn't even sure what she was tracking at this point.

"How much more time do you need?" Rosalie asked, trying as always to keep them on track while holding the peace.

"If we film until the sun comes up *today*, we might

be able to get it done with one more night." Barbara raised her hand to ward off any rushes to agreement. "Maybe."

Jess couldn't believe they'd cut it this close.

"But that one more night is Christmas Eve." She'd blown it. Her first production, and she was over budget and over time, she'd ticked off the town mayor, and on top of all that, she'd lost the guy. Geez. At least she excelled at blowing it. "We can't ask the crew to do that. We can't ask the town to give up their Christmas Eve just so we can finish our movie."

"I can take care of the crew." Barbara nodded definitively as if she were warming up to the idea. "They're a good group of people. They'll understand."

That was one problem solved—granted, a big one—but not the only problem. There were definitely people who would absolutely *not* understand.

"The town won't." Why beat around the bush? "The mayor won't."

Both of the women looked at her as if she'd magically come up with the answer. Maybe even put it in one of those holiday boxes and add a bow.

"So what do you want to do?" Rosalie asked.

"Honestly? Go back in time and stop myself from saying I'd produce this movie." What had she been thinking?

Probably about the already tight schedule and all the times she'd pushed production back. She knew a large chunk of this was her fault. But every decision she made, she stood by. The town was being generous with how they'd opened themselves up to allowing the crew such free rein. She could do no less than honor the few boundaries they'd had.

"Look, Jessica, I know it's rough with everything that's going on. We all want that work-life balance thing." Barbara paused, letting Jess consider that it was life as much as anything getting in the way, before charging on. "But sometimes, something has to come first. You just have to decide what *that* is. What that's going to be."

Says the woman with the children, the perfect husband, the high-power job, and some semblance of balance over all of it.

Jess sat, waiting for one of them to offer a better answer than work-life balance philosophies.

When nothing came, she stood up and stretched.

"I need some coffee. Why don't you guys get some rest."

She'd get caffeine and figure it out if it was the last thing she did.

The door fell shut behind Rosalie and Barbara, and Jessica refreshed her coffee from the carafe Zoe had brought them earlier.

She could make this work. She had to. There was no other option. But she needed to admit that even though she was leaving Homestead, she didn't want to go in Matt's bad graces. She just couldn't leave knowing he hated her.

So, if the problem was how to work with the town

fairly... maybe it was the town she needed to address, not the movie.

Jess threw on her jacket and headed out, knowing there was one person who might be able to help her find that balance she needed.

When she got to the door, she gave it a solid knock, knowing it was past polite visiting hours.

The door flew open, and she gave him her best smile.

"Hi. I'm sorry to wake you. But I have a huge favor to ask."

She hoped he wouldn't just slam the door in her face, but he gave her an embarrassed smile and said, "What do you need?"

Jessica sighed.

That was what she needed to hear.

"Thanks, Pete." She gave him a hug as the older man opened the door wider and ushered her in.

Maybe she could salvage this whole thing.

It was déjà vu. Matt couldn't believe they were here again, having almost the same conversation. It was nuts. How did things keep getting further and further out of control?

Matt tried not to glare at everyone at the Town Council meeting, but he had a feeling he was failing miserably at that.

"Order!" Pete stood at the front of the room, banging that gavel again. "Order!"

That was enough of that. This shouldn't even be a vote. Matt was putting an end to this right now.

"This is crazy." He powered on as Pete opened his mouth to argue. "You can't just decide to let the movie film another night. Especially when that night is Christmas Eve."

Pete shook his head as if this were out of his control.

"If you look at the town charter, Mr. Mayor—"

"Pete, I swear, if you call me Mr. Mayor one more time… Look, any other night, this would be a different conversation—"

Behind him, everyone started shouting about Christmas and the film and why Pete wouldn't call Matt Matt.

"Order!" The gavel came down so hard that time Matt thought—hoped—Pete was going to break it.

"Somebody take away his gavel!" Zoe shouted into the madness, not calming anyone—especially Pete—down.

"Excuse me!" Rosalie joined the chaos and stood up to try to get everyone's attention, which, as Matt saw it, was one of the last things needed to add to this mix. She waited until it started to quiet down, then went on. "Everybody, please listen. I know this is inconvenient, but we'll do our best to not to get in the way."

"But Christmas Eve is the Festival of Lights." Sophie looked to him, waiting for him to fix it.

He wanted to. That was all he'd been attempting to do for weeks. He was trying not to seethe, but the idea that they'd consider canceling the town's "inconvenient" Christmas Eve was so far over the line that Matt couldn't see it anymore.

Rosalie gave Sophie a smile, then swept it across the rest of the room.

"I know, and we want you to go ahead with it." Rosalie turned her attention to the crowd. "In fact, we want to feature it in the movie."

A low hum rushed through the room, but he couldn't grasp the excitement versus annoyance level.

Then Zoe spoke up, asking what they all wanted to know. "Feature it how?"

Barbara joined Rosalie and gave the crowd a tired smile. She obviously had a plan.

"Well, while the lights are coming on for your festival, we want to do the final scene between our movie star and our innkeeper."

Everyone laughed and nudged each other, giving Matt the side-eye. He was about done with the whole thing. And now the entire town's laughter was aimed at him for a kiss that never even happened. The whole innkeeper-and-the-movie-star thing was getting old. He didn't think this night could not get any worse.

"The characters in our movie, I mean." At least Barbara shot him an apologetic grimace before rushing on. "We think it'll be very special, and your town will be playing a huge part in it. And it's not just the town. Guys?"

Behind her, from where he stood next to Jessica, Vince gave a quick wave to the crowd. All the murmuring fell silent. At least someone was going to get listened to—just not the someone Matt wanted.

"Hello, Homestead." He grinned at them, obviously a bit surprised he was the pitch man for this. "I'm Vince, and this is Jessica."

Cue applause. Seriously. Did that guy ever go off-stage?

Look at them, standing there looking all perfect together. Matt couldn't help but notice that they even moved in sync.

"Thank you." Jessica smiled at the crowd, trying to get the applause to settle down. When it finally did, she spoke into the rapt attention. "We're so grateful for all the support you have given us."

Vince watched her until she finished, then turned his attention—and charm—back on the townsfolk.

"Yes, we are. And this final scene on Christmas Eve is going to be amazing. And, guess what... we could use some extras." Vince paused as he let that last statement sink in. "Who wants to be in a movie?"

Matt shouldn't have been surprised when everyone—including his daughter and sister—raised their hands. He'd been trying to protect them, but no one wanted to be protected. No one cared about Christmas in Homestead and their traditions. When it came down to it, they were willing to sell their traditions for a chance at a second on the big screen.

He got up and headed out of the town hall as

everyone celebrated their impending celebrity status. It was finally time for him to give up. Behind him, Pete thanked the movie team for the opportunity and for using their town.

Matt really couldn't take anymore.

Outside, he finished buttoning up his jacket and headed down the front stairs, trusting Zoe to get Sophie back to the lodge after their plan for fame was solidified. He just needed to get home and have some peace and quiet for a bit.

And he was more than a little afraid of what he might say if he stayed in that meeting one minute longer.

"Matt!" He heard Jessica behind him and wanted to just keep going. "Matt, wait."

He stopped and turned to face her, not just disappointed but absolutely furious. This was the woman he'd let into his life. The first one he was willing to offer more than just a passing friendship to since he'd lost Melanie. She knew what Christmas in Homestead meant to him, but that wasn't enough. She had to do things her way at the risk of his town's traditions.

Jessica stopped at the top of the stairs before rushing down to him.

"I'm sorry." What was she even apologizing for?

Blindsiding him with this, the paparazzi, killing their holidays? They just felt like empty words.

"This is fixing things?" he asked, because he couldn't think of a worse way to "fix" things than this.

"I'm trying!" she yelled as if she were the one having her entire world tossed around for a movie, of all things. "We're going to take care of everything. I'm going to pay for the entire festival so you can have the biggest one ever!"

This couldn't be fixed with money. They had come here because the Homestead Christmas was already perfect. Now she wanted to throw around money, offering things they didn't need, to fix ruining the festival?

"The festival we've had has been just fine. It's the one I grew up with. It's the one I take my daughter to. It's the one I took my wife to."

She froze, and he felt as if he'd physically slapped her from the look on her face.

"Oh, Matt." Jessica's voice was softer. "I'll personally make sure nothing goes wrong. Christmas Eve, and then we're done. I'll be gone. That's how you wanted it to be, right?"

Why couldn't she understand that when something is already perfect, there was nothing to fix? And yet, he didn't want her leaving, either. His heart broke a little at what a mess it had all become.

"None of this is how I wanted it to be," he admitted. Couldn't he want her to stay *and* for things to be the same?

He glanced around, taking in the lights, the snow, the decorations, and the beautiful silence. It all still looked lovely, but the quiet was especially powerful since everyone was inside being won over to the dark side. And he really wasn't sure what else to say.

But it was time to return to the lodge... to go back to who he was before she came to town.

He turned and headed off, hoping that when this was all over, he'd pick up and carry on as he had before. Before he could get away, though, the paparazzi found them and started shooting photo after photo—no care for privacy or manners.

He headed down the lane thinking that yes, maybe he did want it to just be like it was before.

Matt continued his brood at home, enjoying the quiet and peacefully watching the snow fall outside the window.

How did he become the bad guy here? How did he start out trying to protect the town and end up having everyone side with a movie crew who would be leaving in two days?

He thumbed a homemade reindeer hanging from the tree and thought about all the Christmases he'd spent in this house.

And now, his wife was gone, his parents were on a trip, his sister wanted to become the next Hilton family, and his daughter was ready for her close-up. Oh, and he'd met a great woman who couldn't understand his life as much as he couldn't understand hers.

Not the Christmas he'd been looking forward to.

"Cute reindeer."

Great. Mr. Perfect Movie Star.

"Sophie made it when she was three." Matt grinned, remembering all the glue involved. "Well, I made it, but she supervised."

"It's nice." Vince actually sounded sincere, and Matt couldn't help but wonder if he'd ever done anything homemade in his life.

"How's the filming going?" As if it mattered.

Vince flashed him a smile, surprising him. Vince seemed to really be listening, not just doing the movie star drive-by thing.

"I have done dozens of movies. Some great. Some not so great. Some I can't even remember doing." He turned toward Matt, giving him another grin. "But this one, I'm going to remember."

Matt considered that for a moment. But honestly, of course, Homestead would be a great place to visit.

"Do you know how our movie ends?" Vince veered, changing the subject so quickly Matt struggled to keep up.

"No." He wasn't even sure he knew what the movie was really about, beyond the basics. That hadn't been his concern.

"The movie star and the innkeeper fall in love."

Great. Even Vince was getting in on the love-life commentary.

Matt tried to keep the bitterness out of his voice. "And they live happily ever after?"

"No." He shook his head. "She goes back to

Hollywood, and he lets her because they both know it could never work."

Matt froze. He couldn't figure out what Vince was expecting from him now.

"That's not a very happy ending."

"No, it's not." He gave Matt a meaningful look. Like a challenge. Like he wanted *him* to be the guy to fix it all. "Kind of a shame, huh?"

Vince waited a beat, letting what he was saying sink in with Matt before turning and striding out, leaving him looking at the Christmas tree again... alone.

CHAPTER
TWENTY-ONE

I n her wildest dreams, Jess never could have expected that this movie shoot would be such an emotional mess. She'd known producing a movie—especially one as meaningful as this one—would have its challenges, but she never could have seen The Larson Factor coming into it.

She just had to make it through the last few days. Most of the time would be spent shooting as quickly as possible to try to get through the rest of the scenes and get out of town.

At least breakfast was good. She and Gavin were sitting in silence, enjoying the best omelet she'd ever had, when Matt strode in, stutter stepped, then kept going through the room without even a nod.

She glanced over at Gavin, noticing him notice. "So, that was fun."

Gavin gave her his should-I-get-you-out-of-here

look she typically only saw when she was in a situation surrounded by hyped-up fans and paparazzi. Matt Larson was a different type of danger.

"It's one more night." She fought the urge to pat his arm. "I'm fine."

She couldn't have been more surprised when Gavin opened his mouth to speak.

"No, you're not."

She was so unused to Gavin voicing his opinion that it took her a moment to reply. "What do you mean?"

He shrugged. "I spend all day with you. I know you. You're not fine."

Now? Now was when Gavin decided to start speaking up?

"So what do I do about it?" she asked since he was chiming in.

He gave her a long, heavy look while he weighed his words before finally answering.

"Decide what you want."

Right. So many things. Was it selfish that she wanted it all?

"If I could figure that out, I'd be fine."

"Just look around." He gave her a grin, one of those rare-bird ones. "You'll see it. Until then, I've got your back."

So incredibly touched she could barely speak, Jessica reached out and wrapped her hand over his large one and said, "Thank you."

To know he was there for her—for more than just the role he was paid for—made all the difference.

It was time to tackle the day. She and Gavin grabbed their stuff and headed out to the front of the lodge.

Coming out into the hall, she was overwhelmed by the rush of people and kids. Barbara stood, hugging one after another, smiling like her day was complete.

"You made it!" She wrapped her arms around a man who could only be her husband, John.

"Of course, we made it." He kissed her on the head as the kids battled for her attention. "You can't spend Christmas Eve alone!"

"Hi, guys! Merry Christmas." Jessica and Gavin joined them in the crowded foyer, surprised by their arrival but enjoying the family chaos.

Sophie was going to love having kids in the house again. It was probably feeling a bit empty with just the main cast and their teams there.

"Oh hey! Jessica, Gavin." Barbara waved them over into the chaos. "This is my family. My husband, John, and my kids, Steven, Sarah, and Trevor."

She shook John's hand and greeted all the kids, surprised they were a bit starstruck meeting her with the job their mom had.

As they all mingled, Jessica leaned in and whispered to Barbara. "I thought you said sometimes work has to come first?"

"No." Barbara shook her head, looking too happy to worry about minor things like that. "I said sometimes you have to decide what comes first." With a shrug, she continued, "I did."

Before Jessica could ask anything else, Barbara hustled her family off to catch up, obviously thrilled at their appearance. The kids were all fighting for her attention as her husband walked beside her, arm around her shoulder, clearly happy to just be with her again.

"That's what I want," Jessica said half under her breath as the laughter echoing down the hall hit her again.

Gavin stepped up behind her, watching Barbara's family drift down the hall.

"Then go get it." Gavin always boiled things down, but even he had to know it wasn't that simple.

"How? I mean, come on, Gavin." Jessica glanced again as the door closed, shaking her head. "We all know how this movie ends."

"If you don't like it, change it." Easy for him to say. "Improvise?"

She was really getting tired of hearing about going off-script in real life. Everything was already messy enough, and that had all happened while trying to do the right thing. If she'd kept to the script, if she'd pushed through on the filming, they'd be done. But she'd tried to "improvise" to keep Matt happy, and look what had happened.

She thought about Matt—about how both of them seemed to have the inability to change what they saw as the right path to merge and walk together.

Laughter echoed down the hall, and she turned just in time to see John drop a light kiss on Barbara's lips before ushering her into the room behind their kids.

An extra day on the set was definitely going to mess with the crew and their holiday plans.

Zoe wasn't sure how much she could do to make that better, but she could certainly try. There was no reason for all those people to pay for bad timing and lost shots. Especially at Christmas.

On top of that, the vibe in the lodge was not the happy one she was used to. Between Matt's angry mope, Jessica's sad mope, and Barbara and Rosalie pushing to get this movie done, it was a little low on the joyful-holiday-energy scale.

The only person who didn't seem overly bothered by anything was Vince. That guy was so easygoing, he was almost a walking cup of chamomile tea.

Matt came in and side-eyed the food on the counter. "What are you doing?"

"Taking some of our extra stuff over to the movie crew." She stopped, wondering how much he was bothered by any mention of the movie at this point. "Sorry. Is this like giving aid and comfort to the enemy?"

Of course, she was only half kidding. Matt needed to get over this change thing, but at the same time, it was Christmas.

"Of course not. It's fine." He glanced at all her piles, probably doing a count of what was going out the door, what they'd need to replace, and what she didn't have enough of for the crew. "It's very nice of you."

"That's what we do here in Homestead. We're nice." She purposefully slid him a look she'd learned from their mother. "Besides, they're our guests."

"They're not all staying here." If a man in his thirties could pout, her brother was doing a darn good job of it.

"Not in the lodge, but they're all guests of the town, right?" She wrapped up another small baggy of cookies. "They're part of the family now."

She knew it was low, hitting him there when he'd been fighting for that all month. Now she was using it to get him to do exactly the opposite of what he'd wanted.

He looked out the window at the town, hopefully viewing his job as mayor a bit differently for a moment. Maybe seeing that he wasn't just a guardian of the town or the people who lived here, but of everyone who came to be part of Homestead—no matter how short their stay was.

"At least the paparazzi are gone for the night." Thank goodness for small blessings. She was afraid she was losing her ability to smile and be kind. She was just so darn angry.

And guilty. She'd known about that picture. If she'd told Matt—or better yet, Gavin—instead of trusting

Ian, maybe this wouldn't have been happening right now. Maybe Matt would be pushing down a quasi-broken heart instead of international scrutiny and home siege.

"They'll be back in the morning." He shrugged as if realizing that no matter what, the Hollywood life was just never going to make sense to them. "Unless some other celebrity does something dumb."

Zoe froze. "What?"

Matt shook his head like it was nonsense. "It's just something Jessica said. They'll stay here until they have something juicier to go after."

"Right." She nodded more to herself than to him. That made sense. A lot of sense. "Of course!"

Juicier. She could get them juicier. Okay, maybe not, but she knew someone who could, and boy, did he owe her. She grabbed her jacket.

"Where are you going?" Matt asked, obviously noticing her insane hurry.

"I'm going to get something juicier."

"What? Wait... what about the food?"

"Do something with it." She zipped up her coat trying to get this show on the road.

As she pulled the door closed behind her, she heard her brother on the phone with the bakery. "Pauline? Hey, it's Matt. Do you have any more pies?"

The big softy.

It took a while to find Ian without the rest of the vulture flock herding around, but there he was, near

222

the dressing rooms. Outside, shivering and waiting for yet another paycheck to pop up.

She couldn't figure out why he was still in Homestead. She'd Googled what he probably got paid and knew it was worth at least heading back to where it was warm outside.

"Do you feel bad?" She knew what she wanted, and that meant starting from a position of power, just like her MBA professors had taught her. Because she wasn't leaving until this was fixed, and the guy who was going to fix it was standing right in front of her, whether he knew it or not.

"What?" Ian was obviously taken off guard... just like she wanted him.

"About what you did." She gave him a look that very clearly said he knew what he did and he should feel very, very bad. "So, do you feel bad?"

"Yes. Of course. I never meant—"

"Great." She cut him off right where she wanted him. "So that means you want to fix it, right?"

"Sure. But how do we—?"

"Your picture is what caused all of this crazy stuff to happen, right?"

The pointed look was not lost on Ian.

"Yes, but..." He shook his head, as if it were all out of his control.

"So, do it again."

"I don't understand."

Before she could scrounge up some patience and

explain it to him, a deep voice sounded from the porch behind her.

"I do."

They turn to see Vince, standing there, smiling mischievously.

Zoe had no idea if she should feel hopeful or worried, but she was willing to take what she could get if he had a plan.

He came down the stairs, pulling out his phone.

"Don't worry, you guys." Vince came to a stop next to them, a wicked grin on his face. "I've got this."

CHAPTER TWENTY-TWO

Jessica glanced around, the guilt really hitting her as she took in the exhaustion written over every expression and movement. They were setting up the next shot, but some of the crew looked dead on their feet. Hollywood Zombies come to life.

Usually, the zombies were in front of the camera, though.

With just two days to finish this film, they had to push as hard as they could.

"Okay, folks!" Barbara clapped her hands to help her grab everyone's attention. "I know we're all tired, but we can do this! You're all doing a great job."

Jessica jumped in because she knew they wouldn't be doing this if she and Vince hadn't asked. "Thank you, everyone!"

She turned to the townsfolk who had volunteered

as extras. They were looking worn-out also, but still showing some excitement about the movie.

She'd seen it over and over again. People think being in a movie is going to be non-stop excitement, but then they find out it's really just a lot of standing around interspersed with a few moments of action. And then, repeat.

She didn't want to leave the town with a bad taste in its mouth—or worse, have people quit and go home mid-shoot. If the crowd changed, they'd have to reshoot everything for continuity.

Don't panic.

Do. Not. Panic.

"I don't know if we're going to be able to pull this off," Barbara spoke under her breath as she led Jess to the side of the shot where Rosalie stood, trusty planner in hand. "Everyone is ready to drop."

Rosalie looked around, obviously taking in all the exhaustion and discouragement. "What else can we do?"

They fell silent, each of them pondering how to pull off a Christmas shoot miracle when they heard the first soft notes drifting down the closed-off street.

Turning, they watching the fatigued crew stop and watch the carolers, dressed in gorgeous period piece costumes, circle the square, bringing them one tune after another. Behind them, the rest of the townsfolk followed, carrying baskets of food, thermoses of coffee, and more.

At the front of the parade was Matt, singing along with Sophie at his side.

Sophie waved before heading off with a friend. Matt turned, a thermos held out toward Jess.

When she got there, she wasn't sure what to say. Obviously, *thank you* came to mind, but it was just— confusing. Her heart broke a little more as she realized again how great of a guy she'd be leaving behind.

"Did you do all this?"

"I'm the mayor." He shrugged as if it were no big deal. "Part of the job."

"But... why?" Jessica glanced around at the crew and the carolers celebrating together. "I mean, I sort of feel like we're ruining your Christmas."

Matt shook his head. "No. This... these people..." He waved to the crowd. "This is what Christmas is about."

She felt like she was part of something real for the first time. More than just part of a movie—part of a family. "Can I ask you something?"

"Sure."

"If I wasn't me... I mean, if I wasn't 'Jessica McEllis,' could it have been different?"

She glanced down, looking shy in a way he hadn't expected of her. The question took him too much by surprise to answer any way but honestly.

"If you weren't Jessica McEllis, it wouldn't have been the same."

And for what it was worth, he was glad for it.

She looked up at him, the flickering decorative lights giving her a halo and highlighting her sadness as she gave him a sweet, sad smile.

"Merry Christmas, Matt."

"Merry Christmas, Jessica."

He tried to think of something else to say. If nothing else, she'd brought him the ability to look beyond himself and his death grip on keeping things as they were.

Change would never be easy, but he was willing to admit that it wasn't the enemy. He saw where losing his wife so young could have made him feel that way, but it was time to move on—not to forget, just to move forward. Life had too many opportunities he might not only be missing, but also keeping Sophie from, to stay standing still in time.

"Hey, Jessica!" Sophie stepped between them, ending whatever else he could say. Probably for the best. "Do you want a Christmas cookie?"

Jess turned that sunny smile of hers on his daughter, always meeting her joy-for-joy. He still wasn't over how she'd handled the questions Sophie'd had about Melanie. It had amazed him.

He never would have thought that someone so disconnected from the real world and without children would be able to do that. But that was Jessica. So much heart, so much to give.

And Sophie adored her.

It was hard to stand there, looking at the woman with

his daughter, feeling his heart in his throat, thinking of the what-ifs that were really never-would-bes.

"Yes, I do. Thank you." She took her cookie and gave Sophie a squeeze. "And a hug. You're the best."

"Jessica, I wanted to show you something." Sophie grabbed her hand and started to pull her away.

Matt watched her go, the end of what was probably their last moment alone, a thing of the past. But her smile made up for it, because he could see what he hadn't in the beginning. That there was Jessica the star and Jessica the woman, and only one could smile with that much joy.

Had he been too rash? Maybe if he—

"Well, this is good news, Mr. Mayor." Pete stepped between them, cutting off his view of her and interrupting wherever it was he was letting his thoughts take him.

"What is?" Matt was still distracted but trying to catch up.

"Looks like your little 'scandal' is going to be forgotten now that Jessica McEllis is moving on." Pete looked more than pleased at the idea of their small town not having a scandal any more.

Not that a kiss was a scandal, but…

Moving on?

"What are you talking about?" Matt asked.

"Here."

Pete's phone lit up with a picture of Vince kissing Jessica. Matt glanced at the background and, well, at least it wasn't at Homestead Lodge. It might have been one of their houses, but either way, the headline was clear enough.

Exclusive: Jessica and Vince Reunite!

His gut tightened like he'd been punched and couldn't catch his breath. That was that. Matt handed the phone back. He felt... stupid. It seemed to be a theme for him this week.

"That's certainly a relief." Pete pocketed the phone, obviously done with it now that he'd gotten to be the messenger. "Isn't it?"

"Yeah." Matt glanced again across the crowd, his gaze naturally landing on Jessica, smiling and laughing with Sophie and a bunch of women. "It sure is."

Bittersweet. It was a word she'd seen in plenty of scripts but hadn't really understood the full meaning of until tonight. Their last night of the shoot.

The last night in Homestead.

It was the Christmas Eve Festival of Lights, and the shoot was going to capture all of it and the beauty of the holidays in Homestead as best they could, sharing this amazing town with the world.

Jess watched as Barbara gave her and Vince their last marks then talked to the townspeople who had shown up to be extras about their job.

As usual, everyone was having a good time. Well, maybe not everyone. She was counting down the minutes until it was over.

Then she could leave.

Then she'd *have* to leave.

"Okay, everyone, let's do a quick run-through. This is just a walk-through, but everyone, act like you would if we were really shooting." Barbara came back around to them and was setting up their last shot. "Jessica and Vince, the camera circles you so we can see all the lights coming on around the square. Our extras start crossing in the background, the first lights come on, and the camera is moving. And cue Vince…"

She watched Vince shake himself off and step into his character. Before she knew it, he was there and speaking his next line.

"You can stay," his character urged. "Stay here with me."

She followed him, right into her character. "There's nothing here for me."

"I'm here. Isn't that enough?"

Offscreen, Barbara shouted. "And more lights come on."

The lights flickered around them as if magical, just like everything else in Homestead.

"There's no such thing as a Christmas miracle," Jessica's character insisted.

"There is if we make them happen. I love you." He took her hand and she had a flashback of earlier this week when he'd said he was in love with her. Pushing the memory away, she followed direction, stepping closer and putting her hand on his cheek.

It was hard to tell, but Vince seemed to almost be telling her goodbye as much as his character was.

"And I love you," she said. "But sometimes we have to let go of the things we love before the very act of loving them becomes too much to bear."

She held out the look, remembering what it was like to stand in suspension when real life would let you walk away.

Behind her, Barbara gave camera one timing details. "And they kiss, and the final lights go on, and she leaves."

They held the moment—no kissing in front of all her new friends for no reason since it was just a walk-through.

"And..." Barbara watched the director's screen for a moment before calling the okay. "Perfect. We should be ready soon. We'll get this all set to shoot tonight."

Barbara rushed off to consult with the cameraman, leaving Vince and Jess behind.

"Man." Vince shook his head as he stepped away from Jess, giving her a normal amount of space instead of standing in their movie close-up zone. "I hadn't realized how much of a bummer this ending is."

"Yeah. We're not doing a romantic comedy where everybody lives happily ever after."

Just like real life. And still, Vince was right. Total bummer.

"Oh, that's true. Really, really true." He nodded, and then stopped as though struck with a sudden thought.

Jessica was completely used to not trusting any of Vince's "sudden thoughts," so she went on high alert.

"But maybe they do." Vince looked down at her, then away, his gaze focused off in the distance. "After the movie, maybe they both realize how dumb they are and wind up together."

Uh-huh.

"How very sentimental of you," she said, watching him in her peripheral vision.

"Yeah." He nodded again as if very proud of himself. "Even I have my moments. Which reminds me, you haven't said anything about your Christmas present."

"What do you mean?"

He froze, turning toward her with a bit of excitement on his face. No one did childlike excitement like Vince.

"You haven't seen it? I can't believe you haven't seen it." He handed her his phone, the screen lit up with—

"What! What did you do?" How could he do this?

He'd said he'd deleted that picture of him catching her with a kiss at their planning meeting weeks ago. Obviously, he hadn't, and now it was all over the internet. Not only that, but every news outlet ever invented had decided to comment on their supposed relationship.

Most of them were excited, but a few weren't being as kind as usual because of her *kiss* with Matt. Only she could get on the gossip pages for two kisses that didn't even happen.

What would Matt think? He'd probably be thinking she was one of those bored starlets playing around on location just like one heard about. She'd never be able to convince him that what she felt was real—even if she was leaving.

It only mattered because she didn't want to hurt him, and she was pretty sure that not only had she done so already, but that this would be yet another nail in their coffin.

As if it needed another one.

"I had Ian Carter help me sell that photo to the tabloids along with the story that we're dating again. You would not believe all the hoops involved to sell a photo of yourself." He glanced down at the phone and shook his head. "You'd think it would be a lot easier."

How could Vince do that? He was not a thoughtless person. Oblivious sometimes, but not thoughtless. She'd never seen him do anything to hurt someone like this before.

"Why would you do this?"

The tone of her voice must not have been giving him the equal excitement he'd shown, because he paused and looked up. She was shocked to see the compassion in his steady gaze.

"They wanted the story of who JMac is dating. So now, that horde of photographers is following me all over town—not Matt. And we're headed back in the morning—with them all following us for the scoop and leaving Homestead peacefully in the rearview mirror."

"Oh." Right. Not thoughtless at all. Actually, kind of genius.

And sweet.

"Look, Jess." Vince took her hand, a friendly gesture that touched her heart. "A huge part of me wishes this could actually be true. But just because I don't make you happy doesn't mean I don't want you to *be* happy."

"Vince…" He was right. That was an amazing Christmas gift. "I don't know what to say."

He shrugged because… of course he did. Tough guys didn't get weepy; they just sneaked around behind your back doing the sweetest, most thoughtful, selfless thing out there.

"How about, Merry Christmas?"

"Merry Christmas, Vince."

"Merry Christmas, Jess."

She wrapped her arms around him, giving him a bear hug, because it was true. No matter what, they'd always be friends, and it was a merry Christmas.

CHAPTER TWENTY-THREE

The peace and quiet was different—in a not-different kind of way. It was what the porch swing outside the lodge typically sounded like at this time of night on Christmas Eve.

But Zoe had gotten used to the throng of photographers staked out trying to get a shot of her unglamorous brother.

She definitely did not miss them.

Ian wandered up the walkway from the sidewalk.

"Looks like it worked." Ian stood at the foot of the porch steps, obviously waiting to be invited up.

Like a vampire. Sadly, she'd already let him in once and broken the barrier. She felt like she should forgive him. It was Christmas Eve, and he had done everything he could to fix the situation. But trusting him again would come slowly, if at all.

She was just about to tell him he could come up when he brandished a gift bag in front of her.

Huh, bribes were good.

She waved him up, eyeing the gift bag.

"Looks like all my colleagues have made a run for it." Ian stopped in front of her, waiting for an invite to sit.

"Yes. We are vulture free." Instead of making the obvious remark, she pointed at the bag and asked, "What is that?"

"It's a present. For you."

"For me?" She didn't exactly put up a fight when he handed her the bag. She nodded toward the seat next to her. "Go ahead."

Opening the bag, she pulled out the gift, completely taken aback.

A framed picture of her from several days earlier— the sun hitting her hair and making it shimmer as the snow drifted down around her. But it was her smile that really shone. She was blessed and could see that clearly.

It was a beautiful picture, too. Not a snapshot. She felt as if Ian was showing his gift, and she couldn't help but wonder again why he did what he did. His talent was undeniable.

"It's beautiful."

"Yeah. It is." Ian cleared his throat before pointing at the bag again. "There's something else in there."

More gifts? Yes, please. But what she pulled out was a piece of paper with legalese all over it.

"It's a photo release. Says you're okay with me displaying this at a gallery. There's one in Chicago that wants me to do a show."

Good for him.

"I don't have a pen."

He had the decency to blush a bit. "There's one in the bag."

She reached back in. Sure enough.

"Of course, there is. You were pretty confident that I was going to sign this, huh?" Leave it up to him to come prepared to get what he wanted.

"More like hopeful."

"You are something else."

Zoe couldn't help but pause a moment, not only to give Ian a rough time, but also to think about it. Her. Hanging in a fancy Chicago art gallery.

This Christmas had been completely surreal.

"Thanks. You know…" He faded out as he took back the paper and glanced away. "Chicago isn't that far from here."

"No. It's not."

She couldn't help but grin at him when his gaze swung back to hers.

"Okay… I better go." He rose, looking awkward like he didn't really know what to do. "Merry Christmas."

"Merry Christmas, Ian."

She watched him walk down the same path he'd come up, turn the corner, and disappear.

Chicago, huh?

Matt was ready for this to be over, but at the same time, Christmas Eve was his favorite night of the year. New Year's? That was for amateurs. Christmas Eve was where it was at. Joy, family, community, faith… Yup. Favorite night of the year.

Sticking his head into Sophie's room, he began doing the parent countdown till they had to be out the door.

"Hey. We need to get going. We don't want to miss the festival." His daughter wasn't looking at him. She was staring at her iPad, a small crease between her eyes like her mother used to get when she couldn't figure out why the blender hated her and wouldn't blend things the way she wanted.

And there definitely wasn't a battle scene sound coming out of it.

Looking over her shoulder, he spotted the picture of Vince and Jessica. This was exactly what he didn't want. Sophie should be adult-drama free.

"Sophie." He pulled it from her hand, trying not to glance down and see it again. "You shouldn't be looking at that."

"Why not?"

"Because it's grown-up stuff." And I don't even want to be seeing it.

"It's not like it's real," she insisted. "Jessica doesn't love Vince."

She sounded so sure it stopped him. Leave it to

Sophie to be more up on the local celebrity gossip, even if it did include her dad's life.

"And you know that how?"

She leaned into him, doing the little-kid-whisper. "Can you keep a secret?"

"Of course, I can. What's up?" Any time a ten-year-old asked about secrets, he started panicking a bit.

But Matt had learned that his daughter was a positive soul with goodness in all of her thoughts.

Well, most of them. There was a small competitive streak he was just learning about because of one of the Haileys.

"It's what I asked Santa for." She glanced around as if someone else might have snuck in her room and was eavesdropping. "For you to fall in love."

He nodded, trying to figure out how to handle this. "With Jessica?"

"No." Sophie shook her head thoughtfully. "Santa must have just figured that part out on his own. You love her, right?"

The bottom of Matt's stomach dropped out as he realized that, yeah, he loved her. He loved every bit of her. Even how she dealt with her crazy life. And if there were any way to keep Hollywood and Homestead in the same world, he'd be working his rear off to make it happen.

"Sweetheart, it's not that easy."

Sophie shrugged. Looking at the world through her eyes made more sense than his.

"Shouldn't it be?" She gave him a kiss on the cheek and took off for the living room, ready to hit the festival, leaving her stunned father sitting on her bed.

Because, yes. Maybe it could be that easy.

"Wait for me!"

"Places!" Barbara was making sure everyone was ready to go to get the last shot. "Last scene. Are we ready?"

Jessica and Vince both took their markers, ready for the big final scene.

"Okay everyone, here we go. Places!"

But before Vince could even utter his first line, Matt ran in, right onto the set, Zoe and Sophie on his heels.

Jessica shook off Vince's hand, not sure what to do. Without thought, she turned toward Matt as he powered toward her, past the lights and the people. Meeting him halfway, just out of the spotlight, she stopped, shaking her head.

"Matt, what are you doing?"

"Stay." He looked like he was begging her with everything he had.

She couldn't have heard him right. "What?"

"Stay. Here. For Christmas." He breathed in, obviously trying to find his center, and hurried on before she could even catch up. "We've been making this too hard. I've been making it too hard. I was so worried about keeping things the same that I couldn't see how much better they'd be if they changed."

"Jessica, come on!" Barbara was obviously losing her patience. And who could blame her when they were that close to being done and yet so far off schedule.

"Matt, I—"

"I know it's complicated with your career and Vince, but we'll figure it out. We have to at least try. Jessica, I'm falling in love with you. Choose me... choose us... stay."

"Jessica, we're rolling!" Barbara really was on a tear to finish. Easygoing was gone.

But that shout was exactly what Jess needed to pull back and regroup. Because she couldn't go through it again. He'd rejected her once, and now, in front of everyone and while wrapping the most important scene of the most important movie of her career, he wanted to take it back?

As soon as she was in place, Barbara was cueing everyone. "Okay. Here we go... and action!"

The lights blinked to life, and Vince stepped up to her, falling into his acting mode.

"You can stay," Vince insisted in his character, giving her a second wave of shivers since the words were far too familiar. "Stay here with me."

Seriously, this could not be happening.

"There's nothing here for me." Jessica's character was at least toeing the line.

"I'm here. Isn't that enough?"

Was that how Matt felt? Was she making him feel like he wasn't enough?

Behind Vince, lights flickered to life and washed

the square with a winter wonderland of soft white snow lit with holiday cheerfulness.

"There's no such thing as a Christmas miracle," she recited, even as she wondered.

"There is if we make them happen." Vince paused for effect, his timing impeccable as always. "I love you."

More festival lights came on and it was... magic.

Jessica stepped in, following the script and desperately trying to ignore Matt behind Vince. She'd walked away. She wasn't stupid. It was the coward's way out of having to say no. Of having to take the risk again.

Instead, she raised her hand and laid it on Vince's cheek.

"And I love you. I do. But..."

What was she thinking?

"But..."

Sophie and Matt stood there, just past Vince—the real deal.

She swung her gaze back to Vince and finished. "Maybe that is enough."

Behind her, she heard mad dashes, script pages flying, and a curse that definitely didn't belong at this family event.

She ignored them all, pouring her soul into the next few words.

"Wow. I forgot what it was like to be loved. What it was like to feel like I was part of something. Part of a community. Part of a family. I spent so much time keeping people out that I forgot what it was like to let people in. This is when you're *supposed* to be with people you love. That's what Christmas really means."

Somehow, the festival lights felt brighter—or maybe it was just her.

Vince was smiling at her now, encouraging her as she went so far off-script that he knew what she was really saying. There was no way he couldn't know.

"Ask me again."

"Ask you…" Vince drew it out, trying to catch up with the curveball Jess had thrown his way.

Well, it served him right. He'd always given her a rough time for never improvising.

"There's only one thing I want for Christmas, and that's for you to ask me again. Take a chance… don't plan… don't think… just act. Ask me to stay."

And then, because he really was one of the good guys, he knew exactly what to say, even though she wasn't giving him the chance for real, he said what anyone—character or real woman—would want to hear.

"I'll ask you over and over and over again until you say yes. Stay with me."

"Yes!" And because the moment really did call for it, she leapt straight into Vince's arms, and he lifted her up and spun her around because that's what heroes do.

They catch you.

"Cut!" Barbara sounded ecstatic… maybe a tad surprised, but still, ecstatic.

The cheer around them was insane. It was like doing live theater but still having to deal with the cameras… and a crazy rush!

"That was incredible!" Vince set her down, smiling like a proud papa. "Jessica, you improvised!"

"I know! Let's do it again." She was in the moment, but thinking bigger, too. "But this time, I think you should kiss me. I think it should end with a kiss."

Vince nodded, giving her arm a squeeze. "I think it will."

When he stepped aside, Matt was there, smiling down at her as she pushed back her tears.

"Ask me again," she whispered.

This leading man needed no help finding his new line. "Stay."

"Yes!"

She couldn't stop smiling, even as he leaned in and kissed her, right there in front of the entire town, her cast, and the crew.

Sophie broke free from her aunt and rushed over to wrap her arms around them.

"I knew you'd say yes!"

Jessica looked from Sophie to Matt and told the truth from her heart. "How could I say no?"

EPILOGUE

One Year Later

Matt couldn't be prouder if he'd made the movie himself.

Of course, he'd been a complete pain in the butt of the producer, as his girlfriend liked to remind him.

But as they finished the special premiere of *A Holiday Homecoming*, he couldn't help but remember that this story had been what had brought them together.

He leaned over and kissed her as the credits rolled, knowing they were about to be hit with the telltale sign of paparazzi and their constant flashes. But inside the theater—especially here in Homestead—they were safe.

On his other side, Sophie was all but bouncing in her chair.

"That was great!" She leaned around him so she

could see Jessica. "Did you see the scene I was in? I was a natural."

Sophie had managed to get herself in the background of the ice skating scene doing a little twirl. Barbara had promised Jessica she'd find something cute and special that Sophie was in, and she definitely had.

Matt was struggling with the fact that Sophie was getting emails from other girls her age who were "fans" of hers now that she was being photographed out and about with Jessica.

"You sure were." Jessica and Sophie had become even closer over the last year.

The two were as different as night and day but connected in a way that Matt was occasionally envious of. Nothing pleased him more than Sophie having another strong woman in her life, but there were things she went to Jessica for now that she would have talked to him about a year before.

And Jessica loved having "girl time" with Sophie when he wasn't even invited. Sure, some of those involved nails and hair and stuff, but still... others were just hang-out time, and he wouldn't mind being the third wheel on those days.

As the credits finished and the lights came up, everyone around them rose, clapping and shouting. He was betting it was probably the oddest premiere Jessica had been to. The theater was filled with people who had helped make it all possible there in Homestead— the town council, the carolers, and the townspeople.

It was a nice change from the L.A. premieres where

everyone was dressed to the nines and networking to get their next gig. Matt had gone with Jessica to Vince's other movie out this year and had been tempted to find a dark closet to lie down in before they even made it from the limo to the theater.

Jessica reached out to take his hand, giving it a squeeze as if he needed the support tonight more than she did. She'd come into her own in the last year, and this was just one more example.

It had been a year of change, and Matt was learning to live with that—especially since it meant that Jessica had a small house with a tall fence just a few doors down from the lodge.

"Jessica, that was wonderful!" Pete leaned over the empty seats between them, reaching out to shake her hand.

Even Pete had gotten used to having America's Sweetheart living down the street. And in return, Jessica had convinced him to stop calling Matt "Mr. Mayor."

"Thanks, Pete." She grinned up at him. "As you know, it was a town effort. We couldn't have done it without all of Homestead."

Pete went back to his blushing over being included in such a big thing.

They moved out into the aisle, running into Vince, who was there with a young artist he'd been dating since Ian had introduced them during his gallery showing in Chicago. Valerie was bringing out the best in Vince. She obviously loved him but didn't necessary love the obviousness he chose to wrap himself in when pulling his "Movie Star Persona" around him. No more pretending to relate to innkeepers or brain surgeons because he'd played one on the big screen. Valerie put an immediate end to any acting-to-real-life comparisons he tried to make.

And in return, he doted on her, adoring everything about her.

"Matt!" He'd also decided that Matt was the best guy in the world and was learning to be a little less pretentious. "How goes it, man? Happy ending, right?"

Vince gave him a hard, action-hero pat on the back that showed more camaraderie than competition now.

"You guys were great." Matt meant every word. "It was amazing to see how it came together on the big screen compared to watching you build it piece by piece."

"That's Barbara for you." He nodded toward the front of the theater where Barbara chatted with a group of people while her kids milled around her. "She's a story genius... even when her leading lady improvises."

He gave Matt a wink and headed up the aisle with his hand firmly wrapped around Valerie's as she shook her head at him in his wake.

He and Sophie stood, enjoying the chatter and greeting people they saw every day in town, as Jessica thanked every one of them, calling each person by name.

As they got to the door, Matt sent Sophie off with

Zoe, much to her disappointment. It had been an ongoing argument for the previous month. Sophie had expected that she'd get to walk the red carpet and do the post-showing photos, as well.

Matt and Jessica had been very clear that was not going to happen.

While Matt had come to accept photos were going to be part of their lives, he also wasn't going to line up the shots for them.

They got to the lobby where the front doors had been cordoned off as Vince and Valerie went through, Vince waving to the paparazzi like they were long-lost friends he hadn't seen in ages.

Matt watched Valerie step back and let Vince take some photos alone while he pointed and waved, all the while charming the photographers who shot questions at him like it was a world leader summit, not a movie premiere.

"Are you ready?" Jessica asked, a small smile on her lips.

"Sure. Yeah, of course." Matt glanced out at the lights flashing as picture after picture was taken of Vince and Valerie.

"You're totally lying and I love you for it." She stood on her tiptoes and kissed him on the cheek just like the kiss a year ago that had sparked the plague of paparazzi who had taken over Homestead for one very long week.

These days, it was known that the sheriff didn't

take kindly to uninvited photographers. The town stayed fairly quiet because of that.

Rosalie waited at the door, counting down the time, and then gave the handler outside the nod. As she led Vince and Valerie away, Rosalie turned to them. "Ready, guys?"

"Sure," Matt repeated, then rolled his eyes when both women laughed at him.

Rosalie stepped forward and pushed the door open. Matt held it for Jessica, her hand wrapped firmly in his as they ventured out into the chaos.

"Jessica! Jessica!" The shout came from every direction as she raised her free hand and waved. They stood together a moment, then she turned and smiled up at him.

He counted to twenty, just as Rosalie had instructed him, then gave her a kiss on the cheek and headed down the very short red carpet to the carriage waiting.

He stood with Zoe, Sophie, and Ian as he watched Jessica work the crowd, the photographers eating out of her hand.

"I do not envy them." Ian shook his head as he draped an arm around Zoe's shoulders. "Not even a bit. Struggling artist is the new job description for me."

"Struggling?" Zoe elbowed him in the ribs. "You made a small fortune off my brother."

"Yeah, but my bank account is irrelevant."

It was an ongoing squabble between the two, but Matt could tell neither of them meant anything by it. And Ian had gone hardcore in making a new life, so

Matt had let it go. The movie shoot and the chaos Ian's photograph had caused had taught him how to keep Sophie out of the spotlight.

As he watched, Jessica sashayed down the carpeted sidewalk to meet them at the edge where a carriage awaited them for their not-so-quick getaway to the closed after-party.

He lifted Sophie in, letting her swish her fancy party dress as she hopped up. Then, as Jessica joined them, he handed her up before joining his girls.

As the carriage pulled away from the Homestead Theater, Matt tucked a blanket around Jessica's legs and wrapped an arm around her.

They enjoyed the silence for a long moment, but when the carriage turned left to go around the square, Jessica gave him a look.

"I thought we might like a little privacy for a few moments."

"Oh, nice." She grinned and let her head fall back against his shoulder.

"Also, Sophie and I have something we want to ask you." Matt reached into his jacket pocket, invigorated and scared to death at the same time.

Across from them, Sophie practically vibrated on the rear-facing bench. But it was Jessica who had his full attention as she stilled.

Matt shifted to kneel before her, not surprised at all when Sophie jumped down and wrapped her arms around his neck so she could see over his shoulder.

"Jessica McEllis, I never thought I'd love another

woman again. I didn't think I'd let someone into not only my life, but Sophie's. Then you came along and blew up everything that seemed safe and normal and sane and brought joy and hope and love." He squeezed her hand, taking the tears slipping down her cheeks as a good sign. "Sophie and I have talked about it, and we love you more than you can know. We want you to be part of our family—our forever family."

"Oh. I…" Jessica struggled to say something else, but the tears were falling too fast.

"Will you marry us?"

"Say yes!" Sophie shouted in his ear.

He smiled, knowing it was important for her to be part of this. "Yes, say yes."

Jessica reached her free hand out to grab one of Sophie's, pulling them both to her so she could hug them together, and gave the only answer he'd allowed himself to hope for.

The one word that meant more than any other.

"Yes!"

SNOWFLAKE CHERRY PIE

A Hallmark Original Recipe

In *Christmas in Homestead*, Matt and his sister Zoe discuss how he's falling for Jessica… and then bicker over a slice of cherry pie. Here's a recipe for a cherry pie that's as good as the ones from Pauline's bakery in the story. Actually, it might even be a little better…

Yield: 1 (9-inch) deep-dish pie (12 servings)
Prep Time: 45 minutes
Bake Time: 70 minutes
Total Time: 3 hours

INGREDIENTS

Pie Filling:
- 9 cups (three 1-pound packages) frozen tart red cherries, thawed
- 2¼ cups sugar
- ½ cup plus 1 tablespoon cornstarch
- 1½ tablespoons fresh squeezed lemon juice
- 1½ tablespoons unsalted butter
- 1 teaspoon vanilla extract

Pie Crust:
- 3 cups all-purpose flour
- 1 tablespoon sugar
- 1 teaspoon kosher salt
- 1½ sticks (12 tablespoons) unsalted butter, chilled, cut into pieces
- 1/3 cup vegetable shortening, chilled, cut into pieces
- ½ cup ice water
- 2 tablespoons white sparkling sugar

DIRECTIONS

1. To prepare pie filling: Place cherries in a heavy sauce pan; simmer over medium-low heat for 10 minutes, stirring frequently. Combine sugar and cornstarch in a bowl and

mix to blend. Add to cherries; using a spatula, gently stir to blend. Add lemon juice, butter and vanilla. Cook over low heat, stirring frequently, until thickened. Chill.

2. To prepare pie crust: combine flour, sugar and salt in food processor fitted with a steel blade and pulse to blend. Add butter and shortening; pulse briefly until mixture resembles coarse crumbs with pea-size pieces of butter and shortening. With machine running, add cold water until the dough forms a ball. Shape dough into 2 pie crust disks, cover and chill for 1 hour.

3. Preheat oven to 375 degrees F.

4. Lightly flour work surface; roll out 1 pie crust disk into a 12 to 14-inch circle, rotating dough as you go to prevent sticking. Transfer to 9-inch deep-dish pie pan, draping dough over outer edges. Cut excess dough and crimp edges. Chill crust.

5. Roll out remaining disk. Using a variety of snowflake cookie cutters, cut into snowflake shapes. Transfer to baking sheet, brush lightly with water and sprinkle with sparkling sugar. Chill 5 minutes.

6. Pour chilled filling into chilled pie crust. Top with snowflake cut-outs in a random pattern.

7. Bake for 70 minutes, or until filling is bubbling in the center and crust is golden brown. Cool before serving.

Thanks so much for reading *Christmas In Homestead*. We hope you enjoyed it!

You might also like these other books from Hallmark Publishing:

Love You Like Christmas
Journey Back to Christmas
A Heavenly Christmas
A Dash of Love
Moonlight in Vermont
Love Locks

For information about our new releases and exclusive offers, sign up for our free newsletter at hallmarkchannel.com/hallmark-publishing-newsletter

You can also connect with us here:

Facebook.com/HallmarkPublishing

Twitter.com/HallmarkPublish

Love You Like Christmas

Keri F. Sweet

Chapter One

It was going to be a very good Christmas.

The crisp wintery air, the bustle of the crowd, and the magic of the upcoming holidays surrounded Maddie Duncan. As she moved with the throng of New Yorkers on her way to work, she couldn't help but notice the people around her peeking at the spectacular displays adorning the storefronts. She made mental notes about what items were turning heads and which things caused the crowds to smile. The marketing-exec brain never really shut off.

That was perfectly fine with her. With a big meeting this morning, she'd take all the last-minute insight she could soak in.

She approached her office building and glanced up. Giddiness sparkled within her, brighter than the light reflecting off the windows of her brand-new corner office. She could hardly believe it, but here she was, standing on her namesake—Madison Avenue—and looking up at her new place in the world. Hard work and dedication had taken Maddie to the next level in her career.

Dad, I've done it.

Up next—maybe her name added to the company stationery? She powered through the building and rode up the elevators. Before she could even think of new logos at the office, first she had to show why she'd deserved this promotion. Her busy-bee coworkers staying on task through the holiday season lifted her spirits even more as she passed through the cubicles. She offered good mornings on her way by. The holiday season was their biggest, most important time of year, but not even the stress of Christmas being three weeks away was enough to diminish the holly-jolly tidings of her coworkers. Bits of garland were strung over cubicles, and mini gold bells dangled from the green strands between large red bows.

She swung around the final row of desks as anticipation danced along her skin like the hooves of eight tiny reindeer. She peeked in at her new digs, tightly gripping her briefcase with a deep, happy inhale. What a gorgeous view! A corner office bathed in cheerful morning light, space to walk around in— and it was hers. She could put bookcases to one side with an area left for a small sitting section on the other.

And then in the middle would be her beautiful oak desk. She walked forward and touched the temporary one that had been set up until her things could be moved in. This promotion had been coming for months, and she'd been shuffled from one temporary place to another while her office was being prepared. She paused at the windows and smiled as she looked at the crowded street below. A few minutes ago, she had stood on that sidewalk and peered up.

The light pouring through the windows bathed her room in the morning sun. The rays warmed the white walls and the boxes stacked to the side. Her golden ficus tree shimmered. Soon she would have all her belongings placed just so.

She settled in behind the desk to start her to-do list and to put the final touches on this morning's presentation to a new high-level client, a new feather in her cap that showed she'd more than earned her brand-new corner office. First, she'd landed Irene's new clothing line—a line that Maddie had taken from an idea to a high-demand brand. Now almost in the palm of her hand was Hadley's apparel line, one that needed some marketing updates to grab today's shoppers. The company was using a playbook from five years ago and ignoring today's digital footprint. If Maddie managed to win Hadley's account, her name would be whispered through the marketing world and lift the profile of her company, helping it become one of the most sought-after and respected marketing agencies in the city—maybe even the country.

But to do that, she had to impress Hadley. The click of her assistant's heels pulled Maddie's attention to the open office door a moment before Roz appeared. The brilliant yellow of Roz's shirt brightened the room. Her broad, genuine smile was the bow on top. They'd been friends for years. Maddie had entered the marketing world at the bottom while Roz had been assistant to a group of managers. They'd laughed and grown a friendship over pots of coffee and late nights stuck working together. When Maddie made manager and was offered a personal assistant of her own, she had pleaded with Roz to come with her. It hadn't taken much begging, and Maddie was lucky to have Roz. Without a doubt, she wouldn't be here without the solid help she'd received from the woman.

"Twenty-three more days until Christmas. We need to step up our game." Maddie clicked her pen, prepared for any messages Roz may have collected.

Roz glanced out a bright, large window with a wistful sparkle lighting her gaze. "It looks like it might snow."

Maddie studied pages of figures and charts. A new line hit her that she needed to add to her pitch. She jotted it down in the margins and crossed her fingers against any potential seasonal inconveniences. "As long as it stays within picturesque limits. I don't want the weather to slow down sales."

Roz gave her that familiar look—a sharp, raised eyebrow and a glance down at Maddie. "Christmas isn't all about numbers."

Maddie barely resisted scoffing. "It's the biggest selling season of the year."

"It's also a holiday. Can we throw in some merriment?"

Sure. In the stores. The garland and decorations

were cute in the outer offices. And she loved all the gorgeous touches decorating the city, but she didn't have time for all those things here in her working space. "I market Christmas. I don't have time to celebrate it. The last time I got a tree was my first year out of college, and it withered from neglect."

Seriously, how merry had it been to walk into her apartment and find her tree dead when there was still another week to go until Christmas? The cheery decorations, the bright green plants, and the rosy cheeks of Santas all around were simply distractions from her work. They took precious time away from what needed her focus the most. She'd end up knocking some cute figurine to the floor, and it would shatter, which would steal more of her time while she cleaned it up. The traditions people claimed they had and the nostalgia—all of that was just a bunch of talk. People didn't actually sit down and roast chestnuts over a fire. Maddie had given up trying to make it happen long ago, because it simply wasn't realistic.

Roz stared her down with a hand on her hip and a challenge in her eyes that only a best friend could pull off and still put love behind it. "You are not that cynical. I know for a fact that you're downright nice."

True. Look at Maddie, sounding like Ebenezer Scrooge. Honestly, that couldn't be further from the truth. She loved Christmas. But she loved making the magic happen for other people more: the brightness on their faces; the pleased, excited gasps on finding the perfect gifts; the giving—the presentation of it all.

That was her holiday spirit. Hence, the poinsettias she'd advised to be positioned in the stores—but not in the way of her computer. She couldn't do her job so that Christmas reached everyone if she was too busy drinking eggnog under mistletoe.

She'd learned long ago there were two types of people: those who sat on Santa's lap and ate cutout cookies for three meals a day, and those who kept the cookies rolling out of the bakery.

Maddie was the latter.

Mistletoe, however, didn't necessarily sound so bad. That would mean another date, though, and she shuddered. Maybe she'd skip getting caught under the mistletoe this year. She recalled her last holiday date. He'd sat down and immediately provided all the details of his still-pending divorce. Ugh. Pass. It was going to take a while to forget that guy. Maybe she could try again after New Year's when the Christmas rush was over.

Roz continued staring at her in the way friends do, knowing Maddie could share more. Maddie sighed. "Christmas wasn't real big in our house. After my mom died, the holidays lost their meaning. I got presents, but none of the sentiment." She stacked her sheets to get back to work and shook off the woolgathering. "A happy client means a happy account executive. That's the joy I hope to get from the holidays."

There went that look passing over Roz's face, the softness of her deep, dark eyes, the almost pity. Something lingered in her gaze, and her mouth opened to no doubt inform Maddie of exactly what she thought, but Maddie's boss, Roger Warren, walked in and saved the day.

"Good morning, Maddie." With his perfectly coiffed hair and his square, masculine chin, he exuded confidence. His hands came together with a clap, and he rubbed his palms.

Maddie was ready to make him proud and pleased with his decision to promote her. "I'm loving my new office."

Roger nodded. "You earned it, every square inch." He glanced at the space and her lovely windows. "Now, are you ready to dazzle Hadley?"

The smile that danced at her lips felt worthy of Christmas morning. "Absolutely."

She followed Roger through the offices to a larger, more elegant space. Cozy, modern leather chairs were oriented around a glass table. Sleek cabinets were tucked against one wall, and windows on the opposite side allowed natural light to pour in so the atmosphere was comfortable. The polished space offered a friendly intimacy to match the level of care for their clients. This was no cold, disconnected, punch-some-numbers working partnership. Oh, no. When clients booked Maddie Duncan, they got first-rate service, twenty-four-hour access to her via her cell phone for ideas or a moment of her time to help calm nerves. Whatever the clients needed from her, Maddie was there. She *lived* for it, even those three-in-the-morning calls where she'd practiced answering the phone to sound like she'd been awake working and not sleeping.

One day this sleek, small conference room could be a space she'd be in charge of. But she'd need to continue winning over more clients to earn it.

David Hadley lounged in a chair, his suit impeccable. The top button of his crisp linen shirt was open, and he thumbed through the sales information they'd gathered on his company. Nerves tickled Maddie's spine as she took her place to pitch her heart out.

Roger gestured to her as he sat next to Hadley. "Christmas is Maddie's specialty. She's the best we've got."

She smiled and swallowed back her insecurities. Back straight, she launched into her presentation. Hadley was focused, flipping through spreadsheets and graphs that coincided with her pitch. He wasn't missing a single detail she'd applied. He put off a straight-to-the-point vibe. She didn't waste her observation, and she dug into the heart of his business's issues. "Your numbers are falling short, but I believe we can turn that around."

Hadley nodded. "Which is why I'm here."

A man who knew his business inside out and had come to the right place to get it back on the winning path. "The pre-Christmas sales are as crucial to the bottom line as the after-Christmas sales. Your ads need to appeal to the shoppers on three levels." She ticked them off with her fingers. "The holidays, the prices, and the clothes." She gestured at her smart black suit and the soft white shirt she'd paired it with. "Which I love, by the way. When you can turn your marketing exec into a customer, you're doing something really right."

Hadley gave her an approving look. "You wear our merchandise well."

Darn right, she did. She slipped into a chair across from him. "I can sell it even better. Let me get the marketing on par with the clothing."

Hadley gave her another, longer look and then glanced at the plans she'd given him. Her nerves increased as she treaded that precarious line between being too pushy and being the right amount of convincing to show she cared. Sounding like a used-car salesman was never the way to go, so instead she focused on maintaining a serene, confident smile and friendly expression, ready for any questions.

Finally, he nodded. "Okay."

Yes! Merry Christmas to her, indeed. Who needed garland and whatever else? Success was the best gift Maddie could ever want. "We'll roll out the new campaign at the end of the week."

Roger rubbed his hands together. "Great!"

After handshakes and business cards were exchanged, she slid behind her desk and pushed piles of paperwork around until she'd made organized stacks to study through the afternoon. She kicked off her Jimmy Choos and worked through lunch with the aid of healthy snack bars stashed in her purse. She jotted notes to make sure they didn't forget all their options to explore for Hadley. Maddie intended to reach every possible customer, not a sole demographic. Her plan was long-term rather than a push for one holiday.

Customers were programmed to think holiday colors meant Christmastime only. Hadley needed them to think warmth and comfort instead. Give customers pieces to nudge them into seeing the appeal of the bold colors through winter. Maddie typed up all her notes, sent them to an ad designer she favored, and opened the next client's portfolio to reassess all of their numbers and to make sure they were exceeding her expectations.

Normally, Maddie's heels echoed against the polished floors of the hallway leading to her apartment, but tonight nothing could be heard over the laughter, conversations, and Christmas songs pouring out of a neighbor's open doorway.

Maddie hurried past his door before they caught her walking by and invited her in. She only vaguely knew her neighbors. One of the guys had dark hair, was tall, and preferred jeans from one of her first clients. The other was shorter, blond, and had an affection for partnering sweater vests with frumpy-front khaki pants. He didn't have quite the style panache as his roommate. While they were probably great people, she had work to do.

Based on the noise, the entire building had turned

out. Mistletoe hung from the frame and garland had been strung around the entrance. A plastic Christmas scene of a waving Santa had been stuck to the front of their door and hinted that the décor within was as over the top as it came.

One of Maddie's clients had created an ugly Christmas sweater line this year because of their recent popularity. Based on the rambunctious noise, their ideal customers filled the inside. She was tempted to slow down and drop a few hints about where the best sweaters could be found in the city, but she didn't know any of those people and work waited. Getting an ugly sweater ad on the front page of the Wednesday sale papers would do the trick just as well. She slid her key in her lock and made a mental note to email that idea to Roz.

She closed herself inside the blessedly thick walls of her apartment. A rousing round of "Jingle Bell Rock" was cut off.

Maddie pulled leftover Chinese takeout from the refrigerator. She'd no more gotten her shoes off than her phone was calling her name. She swiftly pulled it from her purse. That would be Sam, one of the designers she'd tapped to bring a fresh mix to an old label she was revising. The brand was dying because the company refused to reach a new demographic. Instead of moving with the times, they had practically locked themselves into a marketing mindset from a decade ago.

Sam rattled off cuts and curves and highlights of

different styles, and it was one thought after another. This was the energy that line needed, but Maddie had to rein him in a bit. "It's fine to include a younger demographic, but we can't ignore the Gen Xers."

That generation was their key market. Once they rehit the streets, the Gen Xers would check the line out for nostalgia purposes, but they wouldn't buy if all the styles were reaching toward their children's ages. Teenagers weren't wearing anything their parents picked out and fawned over, making them a secondary target. "Go easy on the red and green. Christmas can't overwhelm the clothes."

Sam laughed. "So no obnoxious North Pole–themed outfits to remind the Gen Xers of what their parents would have forced them into?"

She poured a glass of wine and chuckled. "Exactly. Thanks for your hard work and have it to me in the morning."

"You got it."

She'd barely put her phone down and opened her food when a chime signaled an email. She clicked open the evening sales reports numbers that tracked all her clients and sent the files to her printer.

With a long night ahead, she ate while reading other emails. A commotion in the hallway caught her attention. The thick walls of her high-rise weren't impenetrable, and she looked out her peephole as people left the party.

She put on pajamas, grabbed her printouts, and crawled in bed. The numbers were improving for one account and dipping with another. She marked notes and suggestions to tweak placement adjustments. She wasn't even through that when her phone dinged again.

She leaned over, reaching for her device charging on the nightstand, when the lamplight caught on the only Christmas decoration Maddie cared to have.

It couldn't even be counted as a decoration, really. Maddie had kept the picture nearby since it had been taken when she was seven. It was a photograph with her mom, snapped during the holidays.

Classic Christmas danced in the background of the photograph: a beautiful tree trimmed perfectly with golden beads and red ornaments. White bows were attached to the branches, and presents lay scattered beneath as she and her mom were captured mid-laugh. Maddie brushed the frame and fondly touched a corner.

They were happy, cheerful. Looking at the photograph, she recalled the smells of peppermint, spice, and pine. Maddie missed decorations and celebrations at times, but without her mom in the middle of it, the appeal wasn't there. She'd tried for the first few years, but that emptiness had gone unfilled until she'd finally given up trying. The magic of traditions couldn't be repeated without her mom.

Still, the memories warmed her from within, like hot cocoa. That was Mom's standard drink after a day outside in the cold. Maddie could nearly taste the rich chocolate and lightly sweet marshmallows.

Her phone dinged again, and she lifted it to see what needed her attention now.

Maddie worked furiously at her desk. She'd come in an hour earlier to catch up on her existing clients, so that she could focus on Hadley at lunch when everyone else could coordinate. Once Hadley's new campaign was set and running, she could slow down to normal Christmas speed, which was still a seven-day-a-week job but with a little less pressure.

Midmorning, Roz came through with the mail, and Maddie braced for news. She pulled out an envelope. "There's a wedding invitation."

Well, that wasn't what she'd expected. "Who's it from?"

Roz let out a light, surprised gasp. "Irene Parker."

Maddie bolted upright in her chair. Irene had sent her an invitation to her wedding? Seriously? That was, wow, huge. Sure, Maddie had launched her new line, but Maddie didn't know she ranked so well. This was awesome. The networking opportunity alone was a once-in-a lifetime chance.

"Irene is my biggest client." She collected the envelope and mentally flipped through her calendar. Would it be a spring wedding? That would be a bit tight around the final launch for summer lines, but if she prepared ahead, it would be fine. "This woman runs the largest clothing chain in the country, and she invited me to her wedding?"

Maddie tore open the envelope and tipped her head toward the window. "I just can't believe she would think to invite me. She's the whole reason for this promotion." She pulled the elegant, thick cardstock out, and Maddie's heart sank. Not a spring wedding. A December wedding. As in this month. "It says the wedding is December eleventh. And I'm just getting this now?"

Roz winced. "The mailroom must have sent it to your old office."

It was already December third. The wedding was in a week. Going would be a great opportunity. Snubbing the invite? Not an option. "I can't afford to offend her."

Roz nodded. "What do we do?"

Maddie had to get home, pack, and sort her notes so she could work on the road. "Email her assistant and say I'll be attending and explain the delay in my response."

Roz didn't make a move to start on that email. "You sure about this? The wedding is next week, and it's in Denver." Roz cocked a brow. "And you're afraid to fly."

A cold shudder made tracks over Maddie's back. "I can't let that stop me. I have to go to that wedding. I can take the train. I'll get there in plenty of time."

Her desk phone trilled. She'd get there if she could catch a moment to breathe and reconfigure for a road trip. Roz picked up the line. "Maddie Duncan's office."

Maddie steadily worked to gather her things so that as soon as that lunch meeting was completed, she could head out.

Roz covered the phone with her hand. "It's your cousin, Teddy."

The stress found a pause button, and Maddie collected the phone. She didn't get near enough time with the few family members she had. Being as in demand to her clients as Maddie was didn't leave a lot of time for much of anyone or anything else. "Hey, Teddy, how are you?"

"Great." His lovable voice was music through the line. "I got a new job. I'm moving to London."

Maddie nearly dropped the phone. "Congratulations. That sounds exciting."

"It is, and I'm trying to get everything in order to make the move. Do you remember my mother's classic Mustang Fastback?"

Aunt Vivian was a flamboyant and wonderful substitute mom. She used to pick Maddie up in her jazzy vintage Mustang and take Maddie on great adventures, the two of them cruising along the highway and singing to the radio. They were some of the happiest memories of Maddie's childhood. The necklace didn't hang there, but she absent-mindedly found herself fiddling at her neck for the chain. The little charm at the end was a Mustang, and the words engraved across it were *Adventure Together*. It had been a gift from Aunt Viv during one of their last trips. Not quite an accessory that screamed professional appearance, so it hung safely in Maddie's jewelry box. "Of course I do. I loved that car."

"I've been keeping it stored it in my garage, but now I'm selling the house. I'd like to keep the car in the family. Are you interested?"

Her heart skipped a beat. "You bet I am. Does it run okay?"

"It's in mint condition. I take it for a spin every now and again."

Perfect. "What a happy coincidence. It just so happens I'm in need of a car right now for a trip to Denver for a wedding."

"That's ambitious in winter. I think there's some pretty serious weather due to pass through the Midwest this weekend."

"Better than flying. You know how I am about that." She didn't even like to say the word. "Besides, next weekend? I'll be there before the weather passes through. I appreciate this."

"Mom would want you to have it."

"Thank you, Teddy."

"Merry Christmas."

Roz smiled at her. "Sounds like I shouldn't schedule the train ticket."

"Definitely not." Maddie sank back in her chair, not believing the latest turn of events. "I have the most amazing memories from my time in that car. My aunt took me on all sorts of adventures in it." Oh, gosh. Black-cherry red, beautiful classic leather interior. She could remember every last detail. Even the rumble of the engine that made the whole car purr cast a familiar vibration across her skin.

Roz straightened the paperwork in her hands. "Now you'll get to make a new adventure."

Maddie grabbed her things, stuffed her briefcase full, and was ready to go as soon as their lunch meeting concluded. "But not if I don't get on the road. I'll take off right after lunch. I should have Hadley mentally put together by the time I'm packed and can call you with a plan. We'll coordinate and make this work."

Read the rest! *Love You Like Christmas* is available now.

CPSIA information can be obtained
at www.ICGtesting.com
Printed in the USA
JSHW012012010819
1008JS00001B/1